PRIMED TO KILL

Black Jack Hogan dropped the Colt and scooped up the AK-47. The burning in his left shoulder was intense, and he wondered if there was any lead embedded in his flesh, but there was no time to worry about it now. He crawled along the soggy ground and worked his way around the aircraft.

The four guerrillas saw him at the same time. He turned his weapon on them, focusing his attention on the closest two, and the stunned attackers gasped as hot metal from Hogan's weapon tore into their bodies.

But Hogan was having trouble keeping his eyes open. The remaining men glanced at each other triumphantly, then prepared to fire in a sweeping arc.

As Hogan stared death in the face, he saw a shimmering in the air, and out of it emerged a huge sword. Glistening as it carved through the air, it severed a guerrilla's head in a single movement, then came down on the other man and sliced off his gun arm.

Brom, the red-bearded warrior of Hogan's dreams, was the one holding the sword....

Fuse Point

WARRIORS TIME

David North

A GOLD EAGLE BOOK FROM

WORLDWIDE®

TORONTO • NEW YORK • LONDON • PARIS
AMSTERDAM • STOCKHOLM • HAMBURG
ATHENS • MILAN • TOKYO • SYDNEY

First edition April 1991

ISBN 0-373-63601-6

FUSE POINT

Fuse Point

PROLOGUE

Dressed in a freshly pressed tan uniform covered with medals, Colonel Omar Saddam sat in the back seat of his customized Land Rover and watched the celebration through his high-powered binoculars.

He spotted the young Englishman, taking pictures as the American doctor from the United Nations said he would.

Except for the inoffensive English scholar, only he, his aide, Captain Nuri Khalid, and his driver, Assad, were witnessing what he considered an obscene ceremony. The rest of his convoy of bodyguards were ten miles back, ordered to wait there for his return.

His dark, fierce face was filled with revulsion as he lowered his binoculars and turned to the short, bushy-haired man next to him.

"Did you see what they are doing? Kissing the symbol of Satan. They still worship the devil."

The short, spotlessly dressed captain nodded. "The Yazidis are filthy people who should be exterminated in the name of Allah."

"I agree, Nuri." He checked his wristwatch. He had a meeting with the bankers who had flown into the country, and his scientific adviser, Nis, at the chemical factory, and it was a three-hour drive to Qatir.

Dr. Nis was a strange one the tall colonel thought, never having been able to place the man's nationality by his name. And what strange looks he had to go with the name. The man's face had an Oriental cast, except for his almost-yellow blond hair. But all geniuses were strange in some way, Saddam decided as he put the binoculars back to his eyes.

THE JOYOUS CELEBRATION had been going on most of the day. Despite the ceaseless assault of the hot spring sun, the peasants were laughing and joking. With each passing hour, more families arrived, bringing with them food and beverages to donate to the festival.

Giggling children chased one another, running between the legs of adults to avoid being caught, while their parents exchanged gossip with friends they hadn't seen for months. From the highest point, the Persian Gulf was visible in the distance, but nobody wanted to waste a moment of the excitement by climbing higher just for a view of a wide body of water.

Life was difficult in the mountains, but somehow they had all managed to survive through the winter, despite the harassment of the military government and the neighboring villages, where they were hated. But it was spring and wildflowers were poking their buds through the soil everywhere.

Their religion was different from those who shared their geography. Less militant than their purely Muslim neighbors, they believed in a supreme being, as well as in the spirits of nature.

But for today none of that was important. Today was the Festival of the Choosing of the Bull. The animal had already been selected. Later it would be brought out and introduced.

But now it was time for eating and drinking, laughing, singing and dancing and playing games.

Young men in long white shirts chatted with one another while secretly glancing at the newly blossoming girls. Standing around in clusters and looking like bright bouquets, the girls played with their thin, vividly colored veils as they shyly waited for the lads to come over and ask them to dance.

Old men dressed in black shirts sat on chairs and boxes and watched the young people with nostalgic expressions.

One by one, men and women broke away from the others and walked up to the doorway of the shrine. Embossed on it was a black serpent, the symbol of Shaitan.

Bowing reverently, each kissed the head of the snake, then turned to rejoin the outdoor party.

Paul Timkens watched the celebration, amazed at the vitality and joy surrounding him. The 35 mm camera he always carried was in constant use as he snapped photographs.

The Englishman had spent the past six months wandering through the Kurdish mountains, trying to learn enough about the Yazidis to complete the doctoral thesis he was preparing for Oxford.

He'd helped support his studies by taking on confidential assignments for the Americans, such as the task of keeping an eye on the spanking new chemical plant recently built by the power-hungry colonel. So far, as his coded reports to Washington had indicated, there was no sign they were developing chemical weapons. Just experimental drugs, cartons of which they had shipped by private jet for testing.

Of course, as he'd reported, he couldn't be certain of exactly what they were making inside the factory. Except for authorized personnel, no one was permitted inside.

One of the few things he could be certain of was the fact that, despite reports to the contrary, the Yazidis did not worship Satan. Instead, they sought to placate him, believing that God had given him power over the world after he'd been booted out of Heaven. They never spoke his name or used any words that began with "Sh."

They were simple people who had chosen to live in this remote area so that they would offend no one with their beliefs. Paul wished that the attractive United Nations doctor had not been too busy to join him here. It would be good for her to get away from her work for a day.

Evelyn Thomas was an unusual woman. She had been here several years, trying to reduce the high mortality rate.

He had thought of asking her to marry him, but he knew she was too committed to her work to leave it and start a family. Saddened at her absence, he continued to take pictures.

COLONEL SADDAM lowered the glasses and reached into an inner pocket. He took out the long, silver-colored whistle Dr. Nis had given him. For a moment he stared at it and wondered if he was tampering with the true faith in what he was about to do.

Then he remembered what Nis had told him when he had first contacted the colonel.

"Some men are destined to rule. Not just their country but many lands," he had said as if he had read Saddam's most secret thoughts.

No, his was a holy mission. All that prevented him from ridding the neighboring lands of their heretical rulers was evidence that the chemical Nis had brought him—the TX-133—worked.

It was to be the final test. The well of one of the villages had been treated yesterday with large amounts of TX-133. Nis had reprimanded him for using too much, commenting that it might have too much effect on the villagers.

But Nis had gone to talk to them afterward and had returned satisfied.

Saddam had wanted to delay running the first stage of the test until after the bankers left, but Nis had warned him the drug only stayed potent for forty-eight hours.

Forty-eight hours had almost passed.

AS PAUL TIMKENS LOOKED ON, several smiling young men disappeared behind the shrine.

He wondered where they'd gone.

Then they reappeared, leading a young mottled gray bull on a thick rope. The music stopped and the crowd began to cheer.

Timkens remembered. It was the bull chosen to be sacrificed to the sun in October. For the next five months it would be fed and pampered as if it were one of the children. Then they would lead it back to this shrine and offer prayers of thanksgiving before they cut its throat.

Timkens rushed to the front of the crowd. He wanted pictures of the selected bull to illustrate his thesis.

The crowds grew noisier as they greeted the hapless animal, then one of the men reached under his shirt and pulled out an ornately decorated knife. Smiling, he turned to the young girl with whom he'd been dancing and slashed her throat. Two others joined him in the slaughter.

Timkens kept clicking his camera, despite his shock. He had to record this insanity and get the photographs to the Americans.

As he forced himself to continue, he felt a dull thud between his shoulders. He reached a hand behind his back and was surprised to feel the handle of a knife sticking out of it.

Turning, he saw a girl with an insane smile standing right behind him.

Bewildered, he started to ask, "Why did you...?" The rest of his words went unspoken as his body hit the ground.

There was silence as the stunned crowd stared at the slayers and the slain. Then a young man who had helped lead the bull pulled out an antiquated revolver and started firing it, stopping only after four children had sunk to the dirt, washed by the blood that rushed from their bodies.

Mothers shrieked in horror as several men tried to grab the murderers. A woman grabbed a knife from the hands of one of them and rammed it into his chest.

Soon others joined in the killing frenzy, and a weird chanting filled the air to accompany the flashing of knives in the bright sun.

WHILE THE COLONEL and captain watched with fascination through binoculars, the driver jumped out of the car and began to vomit.

Finally the white-faced man wiped his mouth on his sleeve and apologized.

"Sorry, Colonel. I was not prepared for what I saw."

The colonel nodded. He'd never admit it to anyone, but the mass slaughtering had sickened him, too. He took out a linen handkerchief and lifted the edge of his head covering so he could dab away the perspiration.

He turned and glanced at the officer next to him. Khalid remained expressionless. It was a characteristic Saddam envied and resented at the same time. He wished he could be more like his young aide, hiding his feelings, but also was uncomfortable never knowing how the captain really felt about anything.

There was one more thing he had to do before they drove away from this place of the damned. They had to retrieve the film from the Englishman's camera so it didn't get into the wrong hands.

As Saddam opened the door and got out, he could hear the screams from the shrine grounds.

He turned to the driver.

"Go and get the film from the Englishman's camera," he ordered.

The soldier looked stunned. Not bothering to hide his terror, he shook his head.

"That's an order, Assad."

The driver refused to move. Saddam opened the snap of the holster he wore on his wide belt. The gun was an Israeli-made .357 Magnum Desert Eagle, an excellent weapon favored by Saddam.

As he pointed the muzzle of the huge automatic at the quaking man, Captain Khalid got out of the car.

"I'll go, Colonel."

The young captain moved quickly to the scene of slaughter, avoiding those who were still alive. He looked down at the body of the dead Englishman.

"Fool," he whispered resentfully. "You were supposed to tell the Americans I will have something to sell them."

Now he would have to find another safe way to contact them and offer them the vials he had stolen.

He knelt down and grabbed the camera from the motionless hands, then made his way back to the Land Rover.

While he watched the bushy-haired officer walking back to the car, Saddam thought of how pleased the scientist would be when he saw photographic proof of the drug's effect.

1

The slim, gray-haired man sat on the curved plastic chair and pretended to read an English-language newspaper while he furtively studied the people passing by. A polyglot of cultures and countries flowed through the Bangkok International Airport, to and from Thailand.

None of them interested him.

He was waiting for a tall American, well over six feet and built like a heavyweight boxer, a man who looked ready and willing to fight a championship bout at the merest challenge. His hair was long, straight and dark blond, and hung down to his shoulders. His face was a blend of Apache Indian and Scotsman.

But the most distinguishing feature in the face was a startling pair of eyes. The deep-set eyes were so pale a shade of blue that they almost looked transparent.

But just in case memory proved uncertain, he carried a color photograph of the man in his pocket—the picture provided by his employer. He took it out and glanced at it again.

The American in the photograph had one of his huge arms around a petite brunette, who was looking up at him with a smile.

The gray-haired man wondered if she was his wife or just a girlfriend—not that it made a difference to one completely uninterested in women.

He turned the picture over and read the name scribbled on the back.

John Hogan. It didn't mean a thing to him.

Carl Kroyger checked his watch again—9:00 a.m. The helicopter was late. It should have landed ten minutes ago.

There had been no arrivals or departures at the Bangkok airport for more than an hour. The start of the rainy season had delayed all flights, and Carl supposed the helicopter was having trouble because of weather conditions.

He didn't mind waiting. He had no place else to go, and he was being compensated well for his time.

He reached down and picked up the long nylon bag at his feet. He could feel the Uzi automatic rifle inside through the fabric.

He'd received five thousand dollars in advance from the thin, swarthy-skinned man to put together a team for this assignment.

Carl didn't know why they wanted to get rid of the man called John Hogan, and he didn't really care. It was their business, not his. All that mattered was that he'd been promised a bonus of an additional five thousand if he was successful.

Compared to some of the jobs he'd been given, it was a breeze. And a lot more profitable.

He shut his thoughts off as he checked around and spotted the three local men he had hired. Gripping the bags that contained the Uzis he'd provided, they were trying their best to blend into the crowds. He had checked their credentials carefully. Each was a seasoned, professional killer, trained on the streets of Bangkok.

For two days they had rehearsed every step of the mission—the post they would take up, who was to move against the target and how to create maximum confusion. And thought had been given to their getaway route.

The man who'd hired them had left a car parked outside, its motor running, for their escape.

The plan was to make it look like a terrorist attack. There were still a number of antigovernment Communist groups operating in Thailand, despite the government's denials. It would mean his team would have to kill more than just the target, but the resulting panic and confusion would make it easier for all of them to escape.

Killing came easy to Carl. He found out how good he was at it during the Vietnam War. It was the only thing he'd ever been able to do successfully.

He looked toward the corridor that led from the gates to the terminal and saw the strapping man in a thin, olive green raincoat striding down it. In his wake was a stocky American in a business suit who was pumping his legs just to keep up with him.

Excitement ran through Carl. It was his mark. Hogan. He even had the long, thin scar along his jawline.

The thin, gray-haired man stood and gave the others the signal with a subtle gesture, then moved to a wall of the crowded terminal and knelt down to open his bag.

THE TALL AMERICAN paused at the bottom of the long ramp from the gates and turned to the man next to him.

"Any idea what the assignment is?"

When Hiram Wilson had called from Washington to set up the meeting in Bangkok, the Intelligence officer gave no hint of what lay in wait.

It wouldn't be something simple, like buying back stolen government secrets or stealing an unfriendly government's military plans. They saved those for the full-timers.

The jobs the man from Washington gave him to handle were the really sticky ones—the ones the government could never acknowledge. The ones they turned over to Black Jack Hogan to handle.

The nickname was a carryover from his college boxing days, not from any obsession with gambling. It was also his code name.

Lancaster shook his head vigorously. "Mr. Wilson never shares that kind of information with me."

Hogan could understand why. Howard Lancaster was Wilson's gofer in Thailand, and the most jittery Intelligence agent he had ever met. It was just as well his retirement was coming up in a year. Hogan didn't think the fat man could stand the strain of spying on him much longer.

Lancaster was busy wiping sweat from his face with stubby fingers. His eyes seemed diminished in his pudgy face, lending him a perpetually worried look. "I'll get the car and meet you out front," he said nervously as he started to walk away, then stopped and added, "You'll wait for me?"

Hogan nodded and watched Lancaster disappear into the crowds. He looked around for a telephone. Maybe he'd have enough time before he returned to call his some-time friend Louise and see if she had any time on her hands.

He hoped so. Louise was funny, outspoken and fully capable of satisfying his hunger for intimacy.

He spotted a bank of pay phones against the far wall. As he moved rapidly toward them, he saw two young women in jeans examine him with admiration. He smiled back but continued his journey. There was something about his size and the mixture of cultures in his features that had seemed to intrigue women since he'd been old enough to capitalize on their fascination.

He was about to dial her number when he abruptly changed his mind. Letting the receiver dangle, he obeyed some deep-seated instinct that made him turn and scan the crowd. There was a warning tingling on the back of his neck when he heard a commotion across the lobby and saw the frightened expressions of men and women as they moved back toward the far walls of the large terminal.

Then he heard the woman scream.

A skinny, jackal-faced man in a nondescript zipper jacket was ramming the muzzle of a 9 mm Uzi into the back of a terrified Thai girl and demanding, in clipped Malay curses, that she walk in front of him.

Black Jack wondered if he was witnessing a kidnapping. He knew that public snatches were not uncommon in Indochina, where poverty and crime dominated the cities.

His thoughts were diverted by an angry airport guard who pushed his way through the crowds, waving a 9 mm Smith & Wesson .459.

It was suicide, Hogan thought, to confront a nervous gunman in a face-off challenge.

With little more than a casual glance, the gunman fired a short burst into the center of the dark uniform jacket. As the guard fell into a spreading pool of his own blood, Black Jack felt his pockets for a weapon, then remembered that Wilson had insisted he show up for their meeting unarmed.

Confusion and terror through the terminal. Panicked men and women grabbed the hands of their families and pushed and shoved toward the exit doors, trampling anyone who came between them and escape.

Hogan ignored everybody and focused his attention on the gunman and his now-hysterical hostage. With constant prodding from the lethal weapon in the small of her back, the weeping woman kept moving toward him.

The antennae in his brain started sending danger signals. Without knowing why, the American was now certain the gunman wanted him. He stood still until the hostaged woman was almost next to him. The angry gunman shoved her aside and braced his body as he yanked back on the trigger of the Uzi in his hands.

Black Jack had waited until the nervous killer had committed to firing before he took action. With the ease of years of practice, he lunged for the floor in a forward roll. Above him he heard the burst of gunfire and the screams of the woman. Then he felt the splatter of her blood on his face as he sprang to his feet behind the hitman.

Hogan glanced at the fallen body of the hostage. Terror was frozen on her face for eternity.

The cold-eyed thug twisted around to face the American. His trigger finger squeezed another sustained burst just as Black Jack threw the point of his left boot into the surprised man's throat, then sprang out of the path of the spewing muzzle.

Furious at the unexpected kick-boxing maneuver, the assassin cursed as he continued to pepper the space the American had just occupied in front of him with lead.

An elderly Thai couple who'd had the misfortune of being in the path of the searing slugs groaned and collapsed in each other's arms as the metal tore into their bodies.

Black Jack rammed the edge of his knee up into the killer's crotch. As the stunned assailant doubled over, Hogan slashed the callused edge of his right palm into the gunman's temple.

Openmouthed, the stunned killer dropped his weapon, and the American rammed an elbow into his side, then followed up with a thrust into the neck that ruptured the carotid artery.

While the dying assailant gagged on his own blood, Hogan snatched up the Uzi and turned quickly to see if there were any accomplices.

Two hard-looking men, wearing the jeans and sleeveless shirts favored by street punks in Bangkok, charged at him, freely firing from their Uzis at the fleeing crowds in front of them as they did. Black Jack could hear the screams of men and women callously punctured by the death rounds as their bleeding bodies tumbled to the ground.

Disciplined by years of experience to only concern himself with immediate danger, Hogan closed his mind to the wails of the dying and dived behind a long bench.

Waiting until the two attackers reached the bench, he rolled out, firing two short bursts at them as he did.

With a wide-eyed expression of confusion, one of the gunmen fell backward on top of the corpses he had created.

The other stared at his companion in horror, turned and began to run toward the terminal doors.

Black Jack leapt forward and raced toward him. The fleeing man spun around quickly and started to fire, but Hogan had already dispatched a sustained burst.

The fleeing hitman stared at his nonresponsive trigger finger, then looked down and saw the hole in his chest opened by the American's death-seeking slugs.

Hogan was staring at a gray-haired man who had grabbed a small blond girl and held his Uzi against her head as he jockeyed toward the front doors. Hogan saw the terrified crowds fall to the ground.

As the American moved forward, he heard a woman's anguished cry for her daughter. Then a shimmering seemed to fill the air, out of which emerged a massive figure with glowing red hair. The powerfully built man seemed to be in costume...and he held a double-handed sword in his hand.

Quickly he looked around in bewilderment at the terminal, and looked down at the triggerman next to him.

The American had stopped to stare in shock. He recognized the face. He'd seen it before, but only in his dreams.

For a flicker of a second, he wondered if he was hallucinating. He glanced at the others in the terminal to see if they saw the apparition, too. But they were too busy trying to escape or hide from the death stalking among them to dare stop and look.

Before Hogan could focus the Uzi in his hands at the hostage taker, the mirage raised his muscular arm and ran his huge double-edged sword through the gunman's stomach and out his back, then wrenched the blade out.

The shimmering cloud returned and surrounded the bearded warrior. When it faded, he was gone.

2

While ambulances kept arriving and leaving, a half-dozen Thai police officials stood outside the huge terminal building shooting questions at Hogan—questions to which he had no answers.

At last Howard Lancaster rescued him. Waving his official identification card and promising to have the man with him available for further questioning, he quickly led Hogan to the official embassy car at the curb. Gratefully Hogan flung himself into the vehicle and settled back on the padded seat. Something very strange had taken place, puzzling in more ways than one. And though he had no answers, it was clear that everybody would be looking to him for some sort of explanation.

As they drove away, the sweating stout embassy official stared at the strapping man next to him.

"What happened?"

"Damned if I know. Like everybody else, I was just there."

Lancaster shook his head. "It's been quiet in Bangkok for a whole year." He turned and glared at Hogan. "Ever since you've been cooped up in that Buddhist temple in Cambodia recovering from that attack."

Hogan got some small pleasure from the jumpy Intelligence officer's reactions. "I guess it was about time I brought some excitement into your life again."

He could see Lancaster mouth an obscenity, then sigh.

"At least you'll be out of my hair by tonight."

"Tomorrow," Hogan corrected him. He still planned to call Louise after his meeting with Wilson. "I've got a . . . a personal engagement tonight—one that won't wait."

"No doubt," Lancaster said wryly as he thought of his lonely evening ahead, holed up in his barren, empty apartment.

INSIDE THE TERMINAL a swarthy-skinned man in a light-weight business suit emerged from the small office in which he'd been hiding and walked quickly to a pay phone.

Ignoring the dozens of medical and police officials who kept scurrying around, rushing bodies out of the building, he dialed the number to a small embassy whose sole purpose for being in Bangkok was to negotiate the price of the large quantities of oil their government-owned refineries sold to Thailand.

He looked around to make certain no one was watching, then asked for the ambassador in a low voice.

"More disappointment. Send a message. The American still lives."

COLONEL SADDAM stood at the edge of the tarmac and watched the six private jets take off in sequence from the airfield adjacent to his palace. He turned to the blond man next to him.

"It was a successful meeting. The bankers were satisfied with your progress report."

Dr. Nis nodded. "They seemed to be."

Especially when he had passed around copies of the pictures of the slaughtered Yazidis.

Hans Zeibart, the Swiss banker who headed the consortium, had grinned happily as he slapped the photographs in his hand.

"Good," he had commented. "Soon we will get your neighbors out of the hands of those fanatics who run them."

The Japanese banker had added his comment. "And we can all resume reasonable business deals with them."

Saddam had corrected him. "With me."

The banker from Tokyo had smiled and bowed his head. "Of course. I meant with you."

Saddam's pleasant memories of the evening were interrupted by his aide's appearance.

He sighed. "Yes, Nuri, what is it?"

"The maneuvers will start tomorrow in the eastern desert. Will you be observing, Excellency?"

"No, I'm too busy. You go watch for me."

Captain Khalid nodded and started to leave.

"And, Nuri."

The young officer stopped and waited.

"Make sure live ammunition is supplied to the men. I want them to be ready when we move across the borders."

As the captain turned to leave, the colonel started feeling the chill of the desert night.

"Let's continue this conversation in my sitting room," he told the scientist, and the two of them strolled inside in the calm, thoughtful manner cultivated by heads of state.

Dr. Nis stared at the life-size portrait of Saddam in full uniform hanging above the fireplace, then swiveled around and looked at the tall man sitting erect in a large, upholstered chair.

"It's a shame your men in Bangkok couldn't stop the American."

The colonel brushed off the criticism with a wave of his hand.

"Bloody incompetents! I'll find someone more skilled to eliminate him."

Nis smiled at him. "In case you don't, I have arranged for the American doctor to give the pictures of the Yazidi incident to the Americans."

Colonel Saddam was incredulous. He got to his feet and stared at the blond scientific adviser.

"You gave the woman doctor the photographs of the Ya-zidi incident to pass to the Americans?"

"And to volunteer to lead them to where the incident took place," Nis added, looking unruffled.

"Insanity," Saddam shouted in rage.

"No," Nis corrected him. "Prudence."

The colonel shook his head in disbelief. "We were ready. The drug works," he said, talking to himself. He reached into his pocket and took out one of the vials, then pointed it at the other man as if it were an accusing finger. "We have more than enough of the medicine. Within weeks we could have had our troops across the borders in every direction proclaiming victory. Now we have to delay our plans."

"The American government has been watching you carefully. Did you think you could have taken over your neighbors without their interference?"

"You heard what the bankers said at dinner before they left. Their governments have warned the Americans that one move against me would force them to pull out of vital economic treaties."

"They could take care of you—unofficially."

Saddam smiled icily. "You mean with the agent Hogan?"

Dr. Nis nodded. "The general in Washington wouldn't have relayed a message to the Swiss banker if the man wasn't dangerous."

Funds for the American general had been deposited into a secret, numbered bank account for years by the Swiss banker in exchange for secret information that could affect his business plans.

"I'll have Zeibart contact the general," the uniformed man decided. "Surely with his years in the military, he will know of someone who can take care of this man."

"But just in the event he doesn't, having the doctor lead Hogan to us will make it easier to dispose of him in much the same way we handled all the others the Americans sent."

Saddam weighed Nis's answer and nodded, then thought of something that bothered him. "Why would the doctor agree to assist us?"

Dr. Nis smiled. "Is it important to know why—or just that she will?"

3

As he entered the hotel suite at the plush Oriental Hotel, Black Jack Hogan noted with some satisfaction that Wilson had changed very little in appearance or behavior and made no allowance for the climate at all. He still wore elegant suits with vests so he could suspend his grandfather's gold pocket watch on a thick chain between the two vest pockets. His hair was kept long and paper white—Hogan suspected he used some kind of bleach to get it that light—and his flowing mustache sported a jaunty twist at the ends.

When Hogan saw the cigar the government Intelligence man was smoking, he started laughing, much to the annoyance of the stout man.

Wilson was smuggling Cuban cigars into the United States inside a diplomatic pouch, and the only precaution he took was to remove the cigar bands that identified them as being from an unfriendly country.

Despite his momentary look of irritation, Wilson seemed genuinely happy to see him. Or at least he put on a good act.

"You can't go anywhere without causing trouble, Jack," Wilson said, shaking his head.

"You heard what happened at the airport?"

"Lancaster gave me a full report. Local cops give you a hard time?"

Stripping off his raincoat, Hogan shook his head. "They just took a statement from me."

"Good." A puzzled look crossed the older man's face. "Only thing that bothers me is who the hell tore open the belly of one of them?"

Hogan wasn't going to admit he was still unnerved at the thought that he might have seen somebody seemingly step from his dreams into real life. It had to be an illusion of some kind. Wilson would order him back to Walter Reed Hospital in Washington for psychiatric examinations if he were presented with such an idea, and Hogan couldn't even blame him.

He decided to brush off the incident. "The Thais are a peaceful bunch until you get them mad, I guess."

The man from Washington seemed willing to drop the subject. "Well, anyway, you're alive and well, Black Jack."

The brawny man scowled as Wilson used his code name.

"Hogan, you've still got a face that only a mother could love," Wilson teased as Hogan eased his huge frame into an easy chair. "Even when you're not giving me dirty looks."

Hogan grinned. "And there are a lot of women out there who want to be my mother."

"So I've heard," Wilson commented, and Hogan was sure he had. Knowing the Intelligence officer, he was certain the man had kept a careful eye on him ever since he'd started living at the small Cambodian Buddhist temple between assignments six years ago.

The southerner got down to business. He handed over a folder to study and kept up a running commentary while Hogan leafed through it.

It was pretty straightforward. There was another power conflict in the making in the Middle East. The man with ambitions in this round controlled a small country and had built a plant to manufacture chemical weapons. "They call it Qatir Chemicals Limited, named after the capital of the country. The official line is that they're working on a number of wonder cures."

Hogan knew about the dictator who ran the country. Colonel Omar Saddam, a young military officer took over his oil-rich country in a coup against the ruling family years ago. He was one of many big fishes in small ponds who wanted to be treated like a white shark, but he had a personal history behind him that clearly indicated he was a danger to be reckoned with.

"Who's doing the actual research and development?"

Wilson shuffled through his notes. "A doctor named Alexander Nis."

Hogan found the reason for his involvement on the next page. The dictator had a lot of powerful supporters in the international financial and industrial worlds, bankers and multinational industrialists from supposedly friendly nations who were helping finance the plant.

Diplomatic correspondence from the leaders of their governments had made it clear they would have to move away from participating in any of the treaties they had already signed if the United States took official action against the Middle Eastern dictator.

"The operative word is 'official,'" Wilson commented as he scanned the pages over Hogan's shoulder.

The large man grunted. It was like all of his assignments. "So I go in, take out the plant and you deny having anything to do with it," he summed it up concisely.

"And get rid of anyone who can get it going again."

"What happens if I get caught?"

"We deny we ever heard of Black Jack Hogan. Just standard procedures."

It was the answer he'd expected. Only the missions that called for deniability were offered to him.

Wilson examined the long, hard face carefully. "Are you up to this one, Jack? Only a year ago everyone thought you were as dead as the kids you were with."

The jungle assault was still fresh in Hogan's memory. He'd been escorting a large number of Cambodian children back to their orphanages after a day of fun. An overwhelming force of Khmer Rouge guerrillas swarmed from the jungle and sprayed them with death from their AK-47s.

Hogan wondered what the man from Washington would say if he were told that Hogan had been dead—until the monks from the temple found a way to bring him back to life.

He still remembered the vivid dream—more real than anything he'd ever experienced before . . . in dreams or even in waking consciousness. . . .

HE WAS STANDING in front of huge metal doors.

He hammered on the doors, and finally they opened. Someone came out. A man in dark clothes—looking self-possessed, arrogant and smoothly clever. Hogan immediately knew he was the devil.

Wordlessly the man sized him up, then asked, "Are you back? I remember the last time you tried to get in." After a pause he continued, "Why are you here now?"

"I suppose I must have died," Hogan snapped, annoyed at what sounded like a stupid question.

The man in dark clothes stared at him for a long time, then shook his head. "Go away. As I remember, you cause too much trouble."

The doors closed in front of him with an authoritative bang as Hogan looked on, wondering what was to come next. . . .

JOLTED BACK to the present again by Wilson's discreet cough, Hogan tapped the pages of the report. "Sounds like the stuff I'm used to."

"There's a small complication," Wilson said quietly. "The factory isn't turning out your typical weapons."

"What are they manufacturing?"

Hogan knew from experience Wilson had tried to send other agents in to investigate.

"They claim they are working on a revolutionary cure for schizophrenia—an experimental drug they're calling TX-133. From the little we could find out from the companies shipping them raw materials, we think they've come up with a mind-invasive drug. Something like a chemical hypnotic that leaves victims open to suggestion and mind control. Or just induces psychosis, and provokes a killing frenzy.''

Hogan laughed. ''Got more than a hunch?''

Wilson dug into a huge briefcase and took out a handful of black-and-white photographs. He handed them to Hogan.

The photographs showed groups of corpses. He kept staring at the hacked bodies, feeling the anger within himself building to an explosion.

''We believe the people who were responsible for this massacre had been given TX-133,'' Wilson added quietly.

''How'd you get the pictures?''

''A doctor named Evelyn Thomas working for the United Nations smuggled the film out of the country when she left.''

At Hogan's stunned expression, Wilson asked sharply, ''You know her?''

''I did know her. It was a long time ago, if it's the same woman.''

Wilson shook his head in wonder. ''Is there any woman safe from you?''

Hogan smiled lazily to cover his reaction to the name. ''Sure—the ones who want to get married.''

Hogan hadn't thought of her until the other night. Peculiar Evelyn, who was always desperately searching for some mystical connection, the fragile, hauntingly beautiful girl who had felt the need to take time off from medical school to come to Arizona and seek some answers in the red-rock country around Sedona.

''I wonder if she's changed much,'' Hogan mused out loud.

''You can find out on your trip to the Middle East. She's going with you.''

Hogan's face was a mask of stubbornness. He shook his head. "I work alone."

"She'll come in handy. She knows the area and has contacts inside the country."

Hogan knew Wilson well enough to know there was something he wasn't saying. So Hogan simply stared at him, and finally Wilson surrendered. "She insists on going with you or taking her story to the press. We can't have that. Not only would it make a lot of people nervous, but it would make it more difficult for us to take action."

The Intelligence officer reached into his bulky briefcase and pulled out a folder and handed it over. "This was delivered to us by British Intelligence."

Hogan opened the tan folder. There were two large photographs inside, both of large numbers of corpses.

"It happened in Namibia. An area called Rossing Trekkopje."

Hogan closed the folder. "What's the connection?"

Wilson shrugged. "We don't know. Try to find out." He hesitated for a moment, then made a decision. "The only possible link is that where the Namibian bodies were found happens to be an area where there are large deposits of uranium ore."

Hogan whistled. "Somebody trying to make a nuclear weapon from scratch?"

"It would be nice if we knew before they did." He pursed his lips. "We'd also like to know how they get the victims to take the substance TX-133. If they're using pushers, we haven't been able to find them."

Because the situation had large-scale implications, it seemed to Hogan that it was the toughest job Wilson had ever handed him. He wondered if the southerner knew that.

"I'm doubling your usual...oh, commission, for this one," the white-haired man added, thereby clearing up the question on Hogan's mind.

"I'll try to get answers for you," he said. "When do I leave?"

"You'll meet Dr. Thomas in Washington in two days. A jet will fly the two of you and whatever equipment you will require to a point of entry into the country."

"I'll put together a shopping list," Black Jack promised as they walked to the door of the hotel suite.

Hogan stopped in his tracks and shoved his hands into his pockets as he faced his contact again. "Does Evelyn know who she'll be traveling with?"

"I haven't told her. Should I?"

Hogan considered the question and shook his head. "No," he decided, then added a warning. "She might turn and run when she sees it's me."

Or, he added silently, I might send her packing if she has something else on her mind besides the job at hand.

He had a final question to ask. "This mission got a code name?"

Wilson snapped his fingers. "I almost forgot. We're calling it Operation Fuse Point."

4

Night had come to the Buddhist temple.

Black Jack had been trying for almost an hour to get into a comfortable position, but his usual sound sleep eluded him. He'd gotten used to the thin cotton mat, but this night his two hundred and thirty pounds of well-trained muscle simply refused to relax.

A six-foot-three frame like his was not made to sleep on the small bed of a Cambodian monk. Even though he had tried to do it for more than six years, his large frame had cheerfully learned to make do with the narrow bed designed for a much smaller and much slighter body. But his bones seemed to have turned to lead, and he found it difficult to breathe.

The air around him was heavy with impending rain. The slit window in the wall that supplied the sole means of ventilation found no breeze to catch and divert into his tiny cell. Outside was the suffocating heat of late spring.

Trying to sleep naked had not helped. He had even tried moistening the thin cotton sheet with tepid water. Nothing worked.

He was covered in perspiration, and his thick hair hung in damp clumps down to his shoulder. Another night of tossing until the dawn gong signaled him to get ready for morning meditation.

He wrapped his wrestler's arms behind his head and stared up at the ceiling. He could feel the throbbing of the long scar that ran along the left edge of his face. Even after all these years, it still ached when the air was damp.

Something made him restless. It certainly wasn't the need of a woman beside him tonight. After the meeting he'd had an uproariously good time with Louise.

Besides the good talk, her wicked wit and outrageous comments, there had been enough physicality to sate both of them. At the memory, he stretched lazily like a well-fed cat.

Or was it Evelyn?

But he'd been thinking about the blond girl all the way back to the temple, trying to remember what they had been like together.

During the brief time they'd shared their lives, Evelyn had exposed him to confusing new concepts. Past lives, parallel universes, reincarnation, mystical cults.

John Hogan considered himself a practical man. But he tolerated the mysticism Evelyn had tried to force on him so long as what they had between them was strong and satisfying.

When the war came, he volunteered rather than waiting to be called. War was real. The war had provided him with the kind of reality he now wished he'd never found.

But it had cured him of missing anyone, of being emotionally dependent on somebody else. Too many who had been close to him had died, and he stopped counting on others.

He had wondered what she looked like and how she had changed now that she was a doctor. Then he decided there was nothing to be gained by thinking about her until they met in Washington.

No, Evelyn wasn't keeping him awake.

Was it Operation Fuse Point?

He didn't think so. He'd put himself into a situation and he was going to see it through to the end. Either he would be successful and manage to spit in the eye of the devil again, or else it would all be over finally. Either way, he knew he would do his damnedest to make sure Saddam's factory of death was put out of business permanently.

Perhaps he was just overtired. He should get dressed and wander around, through the ruins of what had been the magnificent capital of an ancient civilization, until his body realized it was tired.

Maybe then he'd be able to sleep.

Without dreaming.

That was his real goal. Dreamless sleep.

Suddenly he knew what was stopping him from falling asleep. It was the dreams.

They'd been coming more frequently. Dreams of battles and of killing. Were they distorted memories of the war he'd fought? He thought he'd dealt with those back in the hospital. The doctors told him he had. He hoped they were right.

Strange dreams of another world and the giant of a man in a strange costume, with hair and beard the color of a crackling fire. The man who called himself Brom.

That was the man he thought he saw at Bangkok International Airport yesterday. The man had been crowding his mind, and Hogan thought there was something a little eerie about a dream figure reaching into his waking life. Probably because he'd had too much free time waiting for his body to recover from the hollowpoints that had almost torn it apart a year ago.

That was the good thing about starting a new mission. There was no time to think about anything but how to complete the assignment—and stay alive.

He heard the ringing of the hollow gong, the signal for all-night meditation for those who couldn't sleep. For a moment he considered putting on his clothes and joining the handful of other insomniacs in the great hall, then changed his mind and closed his eyes. A shimmering cloud surrounded his small bed, but Hogan didn't see it. . . .

FROM THE TOP OF THE HILL Hogan could see the outnumbered Kalabrian warriors desperately fighting off wave after wave of strangely attired barbarians. Less than five hundred exhausted fighters were recklessly clashing steel, lances, battle hammers and axes with five times as many savage attackers, sacrificing themselves to allow the bulk of their forces to escape.

How did I get here, Hogan asked himself and pinched his arm to see if he was dreaming, but his flesh responded in the usual manner. It couldn't be a dream, not even a so-called lucid dream, he told himself and looked around again.

In the center of the battle he saw the huge mass of bright red hair slashing at attackers with a long knife and huge sword.

Without hesitation Hogan charged down the hill and raced past combatants. For a moment he thought of using the Beretta in his waistband holster. But there were too many of them, and he had too little ammunition.

He needed quick transportation. A terrified riderless horse tried to race past him. Hogan grabbed the reins and climbed into the saddle before the animal could panic.

As he charged his steed through the frenzied duels, he realized that there was no way to win this battle.

Another three thousand of the war-paint-bedecked attackers were streaming down a distant hill, screaming cries of lust as they ran. No nightmare he'd ever had could compare to the sight of the charging savages, heads covered with helmets decorated with human or animal skulls, bodies painted a dull black, shouting with the ferocity of wild animals.

He jumped from his horse and tore a heavy, wide sword from the still hand of a dead soldier.

BROM WAVED the howling sword over his head in a circling motion, then, slashing it down with both hands, split a screeching barbarian in half.

The metal chain the halved savage was wearing spilled from his splintered body to the ground. The bearded warrior glanced down and spit at the grayish metal figurine of the strange, cruel god these creatures worshiped.

Shoving his long blade into its scabbard on his back, Brom grabbed the metal-studded mace from his waistband and turned to slay as many of the hideous Jaddueii as he could before inevitable death came to him.

HOGAN SHOVED his way to the side of the huge red-haired battler and jerked the long jungle knife from his belt.

Swinging the two weapons like boxing gloves, he managed to slice off the arm of an attacker and briefly watched it fly up in the air then gracefully spiral down to the ground.

Hogan glanced at the huge man near him, glaring defiantly as the fresh wave of black-painted savages continued to scream their way closer.

The angry warrior was a massive collection of hardened muscles and sinew. Standing over six foot three, he easily weighed two hundred and forty pounds.

His long, electric-red hair flowed down over a torn, bloodstained shirt and pants, both made from a coarsely woven fabric that matched the color of his rich full beard. His huge unprotected head was mounted on a bared wrestler's sun-bronzed body.

Still in its sheath was his krall, the long knife that all Kalabrian men carried, and the huge, scalpel-sharp sword. Reddish stuff was dripping down from the mace over his hands as Brom steadied himself for the next assault. Anger radiated from every part of him down through his arms into his hands and flowed to the circular head of the huge metal-edged killing club he swung.

The screaming voices grew louder as their crazed owners swarmed over the defenders. Hogan turned and braced himself for the imminent assault.

Black Jack looked toward the distant hill. A handsome, raven-haired woman sat on the horse watching the battle. Black Jack was fascinated by her costume. A pair of metal discs was all she wore above her waist. Below seemed to be wide trousers that reminded Hogan of harem pants.

Covering her arms down to her fingers were sleeves of armor, and a short sword hung from a wide leather belt at her waist. Around her head gleamed a circlet of gold, and on her neck, suspended from a heavy gold chain, was a large figurine.

The Kalabrian leader looked at her and spit. "The bitch queen, Raikana. Only the magician, Nis, who carries out her demon-inspired orders, is missing now."

Hogan had heard of both the queen and her magician in previous dreams.

The frenzied vandals were close enough for Hogan to see the savage expressions of blood lust that covered their faces. Each grinned cruelly at some private vision of a personal paradise as he blindly chopped away at every moving object, friend or enemy, and let the blood spurt over himself.

Brom had told him about them. They'd swarmed like locusts out of the dark side that lay past the great desert in the east a year ago to conquer and destroy everything they encountered.

Commanded by hardened mercenaries, the flesh-hungry creatures seemed to be driven by invisible demons at whose command they destroyed and slaughtered and raped.

He glanced quickly at the far hill and saw a fresh wave of black-painted bodies, shouting with anticipation as they came over the hill, brandishing battle-axes, fishhook spears, curved swords and skull-crushing maces.

Hogan could already smell the unwashed stench of their bodies. Brom's troops continued to fight, seemingly unconcerned about the sea of new vandals rushing toward them. Each was a trained, disciplined soldier armed with a sword, spear or fighting axe. Like Brom, they were also equipped with the krall, the long razor-sharp curved knife that was their symbol of manhood.

A fresh sea of attackers appeared at the top of the hill. Screeching loudly like a cacophony of crows, the blackened savages began a second charge.

The two forces clashed with the resounding clanging of metal against metal, accompanied by shouts, curses and screams and the pitiful moans of the dying as metal found flesh.

Hogan kept his knife-sword in motion as one of the enemy attempted to disembowel him with a battle-ax. Then a huge, scarred creature challenged him with a giant sword.

Hogan quickly slit the throat of the first, then swiveled and sliced open the belly of the second.

One of the attackers, a toothless wild-faced man who was bashing in the skull of an already fallen Kalabrian soldier, wore a necklace of bleached infant skulls around his neck.

Sickened at the sight, Hogan swung his huge sword and severed the barbarian's head from his body with one angry stroke, then turned quickly to face the next opponent.

Brom stood his own nearby, swinging his mace wildly at everything that came near, twisting and turning to meet each new foe to deliver a double-handed trip back to hell.

Even though Hogan was fully besieged by men coming at him, he became aware that a figure had sidled behind him to ram a short fishhook lance into his back. With sudden fury he half turned and slashed his short weapon at his attacker.

Both arm and lance fell to the ground. So did the skull-ornamented helmet.

Hogan grabbed the long coarse hair of the suddenly whimpering youth and stared in shock at the face. It was that of a young girl. Her eyes stared up at him in terror.

Hogan forced the head back, exposing her long neck. The girl pleaded with him in a language Hogan couldn't understand.

Dulled by the vast sea of dead and dying men, Hogan felt neither remorse or anger and was ready to drive his knife into her neck, but something stayed his hand at the last moment. Instead, he delivered a stinging blow behind the ear that dropped the female marauder unconscious.

Hogan saw that the red-haired warrior beside him had replaced the mace with his sword. With one powerful blow at the midsection of an armored Jaddueii, the heavy blade easily cleaved through metal and flesh and quickly separated the body into two halves. Hogan stared briefly as the two halves separated and tumbled to the blood-greased ground.

All around them, the crimson-haired warrior's outnumbered troops continued to battle the swarms of brutes who wielded their axes and swords with fierce abandon and used the torturous ramming fishhook spears.

Attacker after attacker fell, and still they came. An endless ocean of screeching savages joyously rushing to their deaths. For every one of Brom's men who fell, a dozen of the enemy died. Still the black wave continued to rush into the carnage, with an almost insane dedication to participating in their own dying.

Hogan glanced at the top of the far hills where more Jaddueii were massing.

Finally he tugged the bearded warrior's arm and pointed. "We need to pull back!" he shouted.

"No!" Brom shot back. "Here we stand. Here we die."

"Then who defends Kalabria afterward if all of you die?"

The sweating, bloodied warrior glared at Hogan, trying to stare him down, then reluctantly nodded his agreement.

"There will be another day, another chance to drive them away," Hogan assured him. Then added, "Start the men back. I'll cover the retreat."

Brom hesitated a moment, then began to brandish the sword over his head in a rapid circular motion. Soon the fast-moving steel created a strange howling noise that penetrated the din of battle around them.

The handful of defenders still on their feet looked to where their fiery-haired leader stood. Grabbing whatever wounded they could carry or drag, they began to move back from the site of carnage, alert for surprise attacks from the black-painted enemy.

"I will stay with you, Komar," Brom yelled at Hogan.

From previous dreams, Hogan knew that the strange name applied to him. But this no longer seemed like a dream to him. He couldn't remember when he'd felt so real, so involved, so full of life. Hideous, scary life...but real and tangible, fully charged.

"No. Get going!"

Turning away from him, Hogan dropped the sword and swung the M-16A slung on his shoulder into position. Cursing the strange fate that shoved him into this nightmare, he began to spray a wide path of killing lead at the attackers.

Brom moved back to follow his men, then stopped and watched in fascination as the attackers were shredded by the burning chunks of metal.

Hogan quickly snapped a fresh 30-round clip in his weapon and resumed his fire. The attackers looked around them. They seemed stunned at the carnage and terrified of Hogan and his weapon. In panic they milled around before fleeing from the valley of massacre.

Exhausted, Hogan and his companion watched them run. Hogan could see blood soaking through Brom's garments.

"You've been wounded."

The fiery-bearded warrior looked down at his side and lightly placed his hand against the wound. He studied the wet blood on his fingers.

"It's nothing." He looked gratefully at Hogan. "Again you have saved me, Komar." Then the huge warrior touched a sticky finger to Hogan's forehead. "I pledge my blood and body to your service."

Before Hogan could ask the wounded warrior to explain his words and the name he used, Brom's eyes closed and he swooned against his men.

A handsome young woman with pale silky hair the color of buttercup buds had worked her way through the field of dead soldiers to their side. She glanced at Brom's wound, then reached into the large leather bag at her side and took out packets of powders, vials of liquids and bits of cloth.

"With your permission, Komar," she said, addressing her words to Hogan shyly, "I will take care of him."

As she worked, Hogan studied her. She was young and attractive; her face was heart shaped and lovely, as though lit from within. She was built like an athlete, lithe with taut muscles hidden under unblemished skin. She wore a loose blouse of thin material, and dark-colored, wide-legged pants.

"Are you a doctor?"

"No, I lead the dance warriors," she said modestly.

Brom unexpectedly opened his eyes and looked at her. "Only a priest can be a healer, Mora," he reprimanded her weakly.

"I will apologize to Sundra this evening," she replied while she tightened the bandage she'd placed over his wound.

"Help me up, Mora," he commanded weakly.

"Rest awhile. You've been badly hurt."

"Rest will have to wait. I must lead the men back," Brom insisted.

Hogan heard the sounds of horses and turned to see two Kalabrian warriors riding toward them, leading two mounts without riders behind them. He reached for the automatic in his waistband.

"Two of Lord Brom's personal guard," Mora said hastily to reassure him.

He pulled his hand away. "You'll be able to manage?"

She nodded wordlessly, but her eyes shone warmly.

Black Jack turned to get on his horse, and saw a cloud of shimmering light about him....

5

The soft ringing of the temple gong awakened Hogan. He opened his eyes and looked around. He was back in his cell.

He glanced at the window and saw it was still night, but he couldn't remember falling asleep.

He looked down at the smarting cuts on his arms. He must have walked in his sleep again, as he seemed to be doing frequently lately, bumping into things. What other explanation was there for the cuts he sometimes found on his face and body, the bloodstains on his clothing?

He glanced across the room. His clothes were on the floor, dumped into a pile. The scuffed cowboy boots were next to them, alongside the sandals fashioned from tires that he wore inside the temple. The weapons were where he'd left them when he flew to Bangkok—stacked next to his cot, within arm's reach.

Stretching, he felt every muscle in his body ache as if he'd been in a wrestling tournament. Or in a battle.

He wondered how long he'd been asleep and checked his wristwatch. Still nearly two in the morning.

He had dreamed an entire battle in less than five seconds. Just like the other times when he'd remembered to examine his watch.

Why had the always brief dreams seemed so real?

He had asked the tiny Buddhist monk in charge of the temple for an explanation. But all Mok Seng would say was that he should restudy the Four Noble Truths of Buddha.

That was the monk's answers to all his questions.

He smiled as he remembered the impossible question he'd been asking Mok Seng every time he tried to shake the tiny

Cambodian's serene facade. He'd asked it again when he'd returned from Bangkok.

"Why won't you tell me how you were able to bring me back to life after the Khmer Rouge shot me up?"

He knew what the response would be. He had waited until the monk's lips began to move, then joined in to make the expected reply a duet.

"Study the Four Noble Truths of Buddha."

Instead of giving him a dirty look, Mok Seng smiled at him. "Perhaps you are finally learning, Hogan."

Black Jack Hogan had been coming back to Mok Seng's temple for many years between assignments, searching for an acceptable explanation to the purpose for his existence. Again and again he had restudied the four truths to find an answer.

So far he'd been unsuccessful.

He let his eyes close. He was tired. The dream of the battle had exhausted him as if he had participated in it.

Perhaps now he could sleep—at least until the gong summoned him to morning meditation.

He started to doze, then heard a faint sound and opened his eyes. In the mist-filtered moonlight that had crept into his room through the window slit, he saw a small hand closing the door. He caught a glimpse of a face—a young Cambodian boy, no more than twelve or thirteen. No doubt one of the homeless urchins the monks permitted to live on the temple grounds.

There was a dead expression in the child's almond-shaped eyes. Must have been caused by hunger, or whatever troubles the young boy had seen.

Hogan wondered if anything had been stolen. Orphaned by the genocidal war, many of the Cambodian children had learned to steal in order to survive. Hogan lived up to his sense of responsibility, but in a country of five million people, where several million innocents had been butchered by fellow Cambodians, it was difficult for one man to have much effect.

He glanced around the room. Nothing seemed to be missing. He must have awakened before the child could take anything.

He had seen other starving children in the war-ravaged cities of Southeast Asia. Girls who were barely eleven "working" the streets to get enough money to help feed their families. Small boys stealing from sidewalk stalls and dashing away, risking being killed by the bullets of an angry peddlar or policeman.

He had tried to do what he could. Most of the fees he received for missions were donated to local orphanages. Between missions, he spent time with the children, which had sent him back to tangle with the devil and begin having the strange dreams.

Lying silently on his cot, he wished the small boy had waited for him to awaken. After yelling at the boy a little to teach him something, he would have shared some of the money he kept in the drawer of the small chest next to his bed.

Hogan started to get up, curious to see if anything was missing after all, then changed his mind.

The urchin was welcome to anything on the table. The only thing he shouldn't rob him of right now was sleep.

CAPTAIN KHALID sat in his personal Land Rover and watched the mock battle through binoculars from his vantage point on the hill. Though the battle was mock, in that there was no outside enemy, just the troops pitched against each other, it was live in every other way.

Tanks spewed live shells at tanks, while six of their two dozen fighter jets launched missiles at the ground forces.

Foot soldiers carrying the latest in assault riflery punctuated the air with continuous waves of death-seeking lead, ignoring the overheated metal housing of their weapons that scorched their bare skin.

Trucks dragged lightweight artillery into position to pitch round after round at each of the two battalions, while shoulder-supported missile launchers propelled their deadly eggs into the center of the battling troops.

Everywhere there were explosions and the screams of wounded and dying men.

The captain had seen enough. The colonel's tactics were brutal but effective. Those who managed to survive the maneuvers would be ready to face even the most violent of enemies.

The rest would be buried with honors as heroes of the state, and their families would receive a small amount of money and a handshake from the country's leader.

As Khalid slid down into the driver's seat, he decided it was time to leave this land of madness before Saddam actually put into action his insane plans to start his own holy war with his neighbors.

For fifteen years he'd lived here, the bastard son of a nomad tribesman who called no nation home. For fifteen years he had schemed and sold Saddam's secret plans to his enemies to save enough money to retire. Almost three hundred thousand was stashed away in a bank in the Cayman Islands, and there was another ten thousand in cash he hadn't had time to smuggle out of the country yet.

This secret had not been offered to anyone so far. The dead Englishman was supposed to have talked to the American ambassador.

It was probably just as well that he hadn't. The Englishman would have demanded a commission. Now, with the vials of the drug, he could slip out of the country and conduct his own negotiations with the Americans.

As he drove the vehicle from the scene of senseless massacre, Khalid wondered what his fee should be.

A million dollars came to mind. He thought about it for a few minutes. Yes, a million dollars seemed exactly the right amount.

THE FURROWS DEEPENED on his brow as Hiram Wilson continued to read the lengthy background report on Evelyn Thomas. Exotic tastes were common in Wilson's world, but the American doctor's were—Wilson searched his mind for the right word—unique.

A flower child of the late sixties, she had experimented with most of the organic drugs of that time. Psychedelic mushrooms, peyote, marijuana, then had graduated to LSD and more-potent chemical combinations. She had indulged in countless sexual experiments in an apparent search for new thrills.

Not unusual for the early seventies, as Hiram Wilson remembered. Even her search for new spiritual affiliations was not very different from the others of her generation.

But she had finished at the top of her class at medical school. Her record as a doctor was spotless. It was her personal life that was worrisome.

She had ventured from the spiritual seeker that Black Jack knew to the darker realms of Satanic cult worship. She was a high priestess of at least one underground church whose cult members were suspected of human sacrifice as their way of honoring the devil. Even in Washington, while she waited for Black Jack to show up, she had spent her evenings attending Satanic rites at several of the more violent cult groups.

Wilson was tempted to refuse her demand to travel with Hogan, then remembered her threat to take copies of the pictures to the newspapers. Too much public attention would make Black Jack's mission impossible to complete. It was difficult to slip into an unfriendly country, blow up a plant and dispose of its management team, if necessary, with a gang of reporters and cameramen in tow.

He would have to let the doctor make the journey, the Intelligence official decided.

Should he warn Black Jack Hogan? He might walk away from the mission, and nothing should deter the successful completion of Operation Fuse Point.

There were too many dangerous unknowns to allow the situation to go unchecked. And as usual, if an international incident developed, innocent people dropped in droves like flies before winter....

6

The soft morning sun filtered through the small window and awakened Hogan. He opened his eyes and glanced around his small room. Nothing had changed.

He couldn't erase this new dream of dead and dying, and the red-beard who treated him with such reverence. Even his misgivings about Evelyn Thomas hadn't driven it from his thoughts.

He turned his contemplation to life in the temple.

All the Buddhist monks who lived there—novitiates and elderly monks alike—were required to meditate several times a day. They gathered in the great room with the hardwood floor and sat cross-legged in the lotus position. Staring into space, they listened to the thin voice of the small, hairless abbot intone ancient words from a scroll.

To a Cambodian, joining a temple as a monk for at least three months was part of the ritual of becoming a man. Most of the monks now in residence would be leaving for their homes soon.

Hogan wouldn't. He had no home or family who awaited his return.

He smiled at the vagaries of life. He'd never intended to settle at such a spot. He'd come to Cambodia six years ago with a squad of trained soldiers on a special mission to destroy a local heroin plant and the senior government official operating it.

Then fate and lead from forty Khmer Rouge assault rifles had killed the rest of his squad and kept what was left of him here until he was well enough to return to his own country.

Deep down, he had felt like an outcast from civilization, with no reason to live. And little desire to do so. He had no family, no wife, no children and no friends, unless he counted Hiram Wilson, the southerner who headquartered in Washington, as a friend.

But Hogan didn't.

Motherless since birth, he had been raised on a large Arizona ranch by his rancher father. Except for his rare visits to the Yavapai Apache reservation, where he could play with the children of his mother's people, he had never had friends.

Even in college he had no one who was close to him, except for the brief time with Evelyn. Most people were afraid of him—afraid of his quiet intensity, the power he radiated, and were held at arm's length by the air of strength and determination, the no-nonsense attitude. An amateur boxer, he'd been banned from intercollegiate boxing when his hammer-fists had badly injured three opponents—and had earned him the nickname "Black Jack" for the lethal power in his hands.

Now his only family was Mok Seng, the abbot of the temple. At least it was a place where he had a strange sensation of belonging.

Away from this remote place in the middle of the jungle, he still felt like a visitor to a world of intrigue and deceit he had rejected. Now he was returning to that world to start another assignment.

Physically he was ready. The abbot had made him devote three hours of each day exercising, gaining mastery over the intracies of kung fu, the delicate movements of t'ai chi, the moves of the sword and the spiritual art of the bow. Day after day, every day, he repeated the same drills, then added new ones until his mind and body pleaded for temporary respite.

By comparison, Wilson's new assignment didn't seem as taxing. Just more dangerous. But the fee he'd be paid was more than fair, and his bank account was low.

Building and maintaining small orphanages for the Cambodian outcasts was costing more than he'd anticipated. It was his way of repaying the monks who ran them for saving his life.

There was a gentle knock, and a soft murmuring of Cambodian through the wooden door. One of the monks was outside, reminding him about the morning meditation.

"Be right there," he shouted as he started to pull his body up from the hard platform.

What he wanted was a few more minutes of rest. He let his eyes close for one minute longer, and wondered. What if his dreams had some deeper meaning? Perhaps he was dreaming of a past life he had lived on Earth.

Then he remembered the twin moons.

No, if it was a past life, it hadn't been on Earth.

Another knock sounded at the door, this time not so gentle.

"Coming," he called. Even here, there never seemed to be enough time for exploring private thoughts, he grumbled as he slowly rotated his neck to ease the stiffness.

Leaning on an elbow, he glanced through the narrow window at the tall spiral towers of the nearby ruins of Angkor Wat.

Founded a thousand years ago as the capital of an ancient Khmer kingdom, the ancient city had stubbornly refused to surrender to the hungry jungle or to the grave robbers who had torn into its foundations, seeking treasure.

The large man stretched his muscular arms and long, sinewy-thickened legs to relieve the cramps. Every morning he experienced the same aches from sleeping on a thin cotton mat that sat on top of the short, narrow wooden platform.

He had asked Mok Seng for something longer and softer long ago, but the small abbot had blandly replied, "Humility is the first step toward true serenity."

Hogan groaned as he tried to unknot the twisted places in his back. Sometimes he wished he could convince Mok Seng he was willing to forgo some serenity for an American-made mattress.

Then he yawned and kicked the thin cover from his body. He swung his long, sunbaked legs over the side of the bed and started to set them on the stone floor when he heard a very faint rustling sound from underneath his wooden platform.

He stared at the floor in horrified fascination as the small head of a snake poked out from under his bed.

Quickly and carefully he pulled his feet back and watched as the short serpent slithered across the floor. It moved slowly, darting its pointed head in every direction, spitting into the air with its forked tongue. The creature was small— less than three feet long. It was a motley tan-green, with subtle markings on its scaly body.

Hogan could imagine it moving through tall grasses or a forest, undetected until it struck.

The expression on Hogan's already deep-tan face darkened even more as the angry reptile turned, lifted its pointed head and stared at him. For a long moment the snake froze and examined him with cold eyes, then lowered its head to the floor and waited.

Hogan knew that snakes had limited vision, that they hunted by sound and vibration. But he could almost swear that this one was looking for him.

This was no harmless garter snake. The hard-faced man had recognized it the minute it had poked its venomous head from under the narrow cot.

A carpet viper. One of the most deadly snakes in the world, filled with neurotoxin that could kill a full-grown man in minutes. As little as five milligrams of its venom was deadly for an adult, compared to the one hundred and fifty milligrams of diamondback rattlesnake venom needed to kill a man. He'd seen the carpet viper in India, when he'd been there on a confidential assignment.

Carpet vipers had notorious short tempers. They struck angrily at anything that moved near them, jabbing their needle-sharp fingers into their victim and pumping their poison into the flesh.

What was it doing in northwestern Cambodia, so many miles away from its home in India?

His first thought was that it had escaped from the snake farm in Bangkok, north of where he was. The capital of Thailand was at least eighty air miles away—even farther on the ground. Snakes normally didn't migrate.

No. Someone had brought the deadly reptile to the temple, Hogan decided. Why? The only logical explanation was that the snake was meant to kill him.

For a long time—ever since he had started having the recurring dreams—he had an uneasy feeling that some evil intent was haunting him, not in the dreams or because of them, but in his waking hours. He felt on occasion that he was watched, spied upon.

"Well, I would think there could be reason for you to have enemies," Wilson admitted, "except for the fact that no one who could harm you even knows you exist."

Hogan had begun to believe that Wilson was right. The government had kept his existence secret.

Except now there was a lethal creature slithering around on his cell's floor.

He stared at the guns. Despite the monk's opposition to violence and weapons, he was permitted to keep them here. They understood his unwillingness to wander into the rural areas unarmed.

Even with his long muscular legs, Hogan doubted he could reach either weapon before the snake struck.

He remembered the long jungle knife and swiftly checked to see if it was still on the hook. When he saw it, he quickly calculated the distance from the bed to the wall and decided he could make it there before the viper reached him.

The deadly small serpent turned its attention to the wooden door, seeking a way to escape. There was a space between the bottom of the door and the stone floor. Angrily the viper tried to force its muscular body through it.

Hogan sprang from his bed and dashed for the wall. Snatching the knife with both hands, he spun around and raised the machetelike weapon, ready to sever the snake's poisonous head from its body.

Then a familiar shrill voice stopped him.

"No!"

Hogan froze his hands in midair at the sharpness of the tone. As he stared in stunned surprise, he saw the slight monk, in his saffron-colored garment, swiftly kneel and grab the spitting serpent behind its head. In his other hand the man was holding a woven wicker basket with a tightly fitting cover.

The angry serpent refused to surrender without a fight. Wriggling furiously, it tried desperately to twist its head so it could plant its deadly venom into his captor. But Mok Seng lifted the cover and casually dropped the writhing serpent into the basket, then quickly sealed the basket again. He set the basket on the floor and removed the small, round eyeglasses he was wearing. As he wiped them on the edge of his robe, he looked reproachfully at the suddenly sweating larger man.

The wizened old man sounded like a chastising parent. "When will you *pnongs*—you barbarians—learn that no creatures may be killed in this temple?"

Hogan was too stunned at the sudden appearance of the monk to smart at the rebuke.

"Thank you, 'little grandfather,'" he said gratefully. Hogan had discovered during his stay that the Cambodian word for the abbot of a Buddhist temple translated roughly as "grandfather" and had used the nickname ever since.

Mok Seng glowered at the translation but kept his silence as he lifted the wicker basket.

The angry serpent hissed and thudded against the walls of the basket as it twisted around angrily. Black Jack stared at the sealed basket.

"How did the snake get in here?"

"A young boy brought him."

Hogan wondered if it was the same boy who'd come into his room. "How do you know that?"

Looking at Hogan as though he were dealing with a child, Mok Seng answered serenely, "Because he said so."

Hogan felt excitement race through his body. "You caught him?"

"No. He allowed himself to be captured."

Hogan was confused. "Why?"

"When one of my brothers found him fallen on the path outside, he was clasping to his neck the mate of the snake who visited you."

Hogan was sickened by the image. Maybe they were dealing with a magic rite, since some of the rural Cambodians still followed the orders of primitive sorcerers.

"Khmer Rouge?"

The monk shrugged. "Possibly. The monk who found him said he kept talking incoherently about a sacred mission before he died." He held up a small bottle filled with a blackish-looking liquid. "He was carrying this."

Hogan stared at the contents. "What is it?"

"A potion made from oily liana, dried python and the excrement from a red vulture. It is dispensed by a *kru*—a sorcerer in your language—in a secret ceremony."

"What's it supposed to do?"

"Protect you from death." The monk opened the bottle and smelled the contents. His usually calm face twisted in disgust.

Hogan thought of the dead boy. "It didn't work."

"Nor did this." Mok Seng held up a large yellow tooth tied to a length of leather string.

The American recognized it. Many of the village dwellers wore one like it. "That's a *katha,* isn't it?"

The abbot looked pleased. "You are finally learning. Yes, the tooth of a parent is very powerful protection against harm."

"I thought only the superstitious wore them."

"I believe the Khmer Rouge's fear of punishment by the spirits is as strong as their political beliefs. Perhaps even stronger."

Hogan remembered all too clearly the first time he had encountered the fanatical teenaged killers of the Cambodian guerrilla forces. They all wore *kathas* around their necks.

He had defied the devil since that encounter. The last time was a year ago when he had the landmark dream of being told to get out of hell and go bother the living.

But he couldn't afford to immerse himself in his memories, because the tiny holy man sternly intruded on his memories. "Get dressed. Then you will go to meditation. Afterward it will be time for your daily lesson in humility."

Hogan wasn't sure he was ready to have Mok Seng make him feel foolish again, but the slight man stared him down.

Finally Hogan surrendered and slipped into a pair of black cotton pants, then put on the kimono the monk expected him to wear at practice and stepped into a pair of sandals made from discarded automobile tires.

Mok Seng gave him an appraising look. "And wash the blood from your forehead."

Hogan examined his face in the chipped mirror over the small stand. There was a long streak of dried red above his eyes.

His face twisted into a scowl as he searched for a scratch. There was none. What was the source of the streak of blood? He could feel a tightening in his chest as he remembered the dream warrior touching his forehead. But the next second he dismissed the notion as nothing more than another nightmare.

As he started to turn from the mirror, his attention was caught by something moving over the shiny surface, like twin glowing orbs, and he stood stock-still, staring in disbelief....

7

The twin moons were making their nightly appearance by the time Brom reined in his mount before the large tent that was his dwelling. He dismounted, and, despite the throbbing agony of his deep wound, he stood at attention as the long parade of men and bodies passed before him.

He looked up at the evening sky, at the multitude of stars. Here in the wide-open spaces, he felt at home. To the south he could see the walled city of Ashankar, where the summer palace was located. Some of his senior commanders had urged him to set up his headquarters there, but Brom had chosen to stay with his men. He had little use for the intricacies of politics and flowery conversation. He had been raised to be a warrior. He was well content to let someone else rule for him until he was ready to settle down and be bored.

His uncle, Draka, and Mondlock shared that function when the need arose. For now the need was to drive Raikana and her creatures from their kingdom. Politics would have to wait.

From inside the tent, a gray-bearded man emerged and silently stood by his side. The tall man wore a long robe that covered his entire body. His long, thin face was etched with age, and his dark hair was sprinkled with gray. Yet he did not look old. His deep-set sapphire eyes burned brightly with the fire of a younger man.

This was Mondlock the Knower, the wise man who had come out of the west and across the mountains of the gods many years ago to become chief counselor to Brom's father, and now to Brom.

Together they watched as individually the soldiers, whether mounted or on foot, paused and saluted as they passed Brom and the wise man, then moved on to the corral where they dismounted their horses and proceeded to the priests' tents for treatment or to rejoin their women and children.

Grimly Brom watched as the large wagons carried the dead to the spot where sacrificers would prepare the bodies for cremation later that night. Pavad, the god of dying, would have a busy time later escorting warriors to their final resting places.

There would be wailing from the women and children. Then the celebration for those who still lived. Food and honeybrew. Enough to fill the bellies and drown the memories temporarily.

He could feel his mind cloud over and realized that he must have lost a great quantity of blood. He forced himself to stay alert until the last funeral wagon had passed.

"There is disturbing news," Mondlock said gravely. "Some of the men saw another party of the black-painted ones coming from the direction of the Forbidden Region," Mondlock said quietly.

"Let them have the region. They will die," Brom commented.

The legends said that poisonous petrified dragons lurked in the rocks of the area and waited to attack unsuspecting travelers. After they had injected them with their venom, they sprayed the bodies with sheets of their fiery breath.

Mondlock gave Brom a reproving glance. "No," the graybeard said firmly. "They must be kept out of the Forbidden Region."

Brom disagreed. "If Raikana wants to save us the trouble of killing her creatures, we should let her."

Before Mondlock could reply, he saw Brom's face drain of all color. Quickly he helped the warrior inside the tent and steadied him until he sank exhausted onto the cushions, then knelt and removed his weapons.

Brom had opened his eyes. "I dreamed of how I first met Komar," he said in a weak voice.

"Try to rest. Panka will be here soon with his healing medicines."

Ignoring him, the wounded warrior insisted on talking.

"Pavad had come to escort me to the eternal place. But when we got there, the sky god Sundra told me I did not belong with him. So Pavad took me to the place of Forever Darkness. Demar, who rules the Underworld, stopped me at the great doors to his castle, and told me he had enough tumult without my presence. Then I saw the figure carrying a fire-stick, like the god of vengeance, Komar."

Brom stopped to gasp for air, and Mondlock rushed to his side, but the red-bearded man held his hand up to stave him off. He regained his breath and wanted to continue.

"Komar came again today to fight by my side," he added.

"Just as you have come to his aid," Mondlock reminded him.

The weakened leader smiled. "Aye, but that was only in my dreams." He shook his head in wonder. "I wonder why so many try to harm Komar in my dreams?"

Mondlock shrugged. "Perhaps because he is the god of vengeance." Then he added, "There is something more important to concern yourself with. The time of the Sjarik comes soon."

Brom had been too busy with the war to remember. The hot, cleansing wind of Sundra always came at this time.

"Will you cease all combat till it passes?"

Brom thought about it, then asked a question back. "Will you leave for your meditation with the gods when it is here?"

"As I have every year," the Knower replied. "But more important than my journey is whether Raikana will cease her attacks during the Sjarik."

"She must. None except the bravest of warriors, protected by the gods, can survive the cleansing wind of the sky father."

"Does Raikana and her Jaddueii know that?"

Brom was about to snap a reply, then stopped. He had no answer. The warrior-queen also the priestess of an evil cult, was a madwoman, and people whose minds were possessed by evil spirits, insane people, did not think as normal men did.

"Consider whether you will be strong enough to lead the Manhood Tests while I find what is delaying Panka," Mondlock said as he withdrew from the tent, leaving the wounded warrior to think about the Sjarik.

THE SJARIK was the subject of discussion in the temple to Raik, which the queen had built in the palace of the Kalabrian rulers that she now controlled.

As she personally lit tall black candles around the base of the black stone statue of the seated god, Raik, men in black uniforms tried to sway her, though they knew their tall, angular queen was very willful and didn't like to be crossed.

"Soon the screaming wind would rage across the plains and hills and suck away air and moisture. Nothing can live in it," a black-bearded captain warned.

"But as leader of the Kalabrians, Brom will be expected to set an example for his warriors and lead them in their absurd Manhood Tests during the Sjarik," the raven-haired woman reminded him. "By tradition each warrior must find his own place to withstand the wind. That's when we'll wipe out the Kalabrian army."

"We are low on men. We lost three thousand in yesterday's battle alone," Karek, a bearded officer, reminded her.

Raikana's face was expressionless as she listened.

She bowed to the statue, then glanced around the room. Her purple pupils burned with impatient incandescent flames as she stared icily at the officer who had dared complain.

"Then bring in more Jaddueii," she said frostily.

"Impossible, your Majesty. Twelve thousand have already died in the Kalabrian campaign," a sallow-faced mercenary captain who had joined her army when they were conquering Tana, announced bitterly. He walked to her side.

"It takes time to prepare soldiers for battle."

The tapered candle flames reflected on his brightly polished metal chest plate as he stared defiantly at the woman.

"Brave, but stupid," she commented, fingering the large precious metal figurine she wore on a thick chain around her neck.

The figurine was the repulsive form and face of Raik, displayed in his horrific glory.

Her officers were aware of what the gesture meant. She was summoning power from the god from whom she claimed direct descent. Someone in the room would die unless her orders were carried out.

She had made her subjects, from commanders down to servant women, wear a similar figurine around their necks, but not of precious metal.

A brute-faced guard entered the room and looked at Raikana for permission to approach. Under his arm he carried a small bird. She saw him and gestured for him to come forward.

Nervously the guard moved closer and quickly knelt before handing the creature to her. She stroked the bird awhile and glanced at the small metal cylinder it wore around its neck.

Gently she removed the capsule and opened it. The reed inside was unbroken. If Brom had been killed in the battle, the reed would have been broken. Draka, his uncle, was supposed to have made certain that he never returned from the conflict.

She'd talk to the magician about a suitable punishment to remind the Kalabrian traitor she had purchased his loyalties by killing his brother, the king, and his wife.

As she considered the best way to have Draka remember who owned him, her hands tightened around the small bird she was holding.

The terrified creature pecked at a finger, but Raikana picked it up and twisted its neck. She removed the canister from its feet and handed it, along with the little corpse, to the guard. "Dispose of the bird and take this canister to the magician."

The guard had knelt to receive the items. Suddenly perspiring, the man got to his feet and moved backward from the table.

"Wait," she called out, and he turned back to her.

"Tell the priestesses it is time to serve the sacrifice to Raik."

Shivering, the guard nodded and bolted from the room.

She smiled as she watched the reactions of the men around the table. They tried hard to disguise their feelings of disgust and fear at the mention of the nightly ritual.

Two sharp-faced women in coarse gray robes entered, carrying trays of roasted meat. Even the most hardened of the commanders shuddered at their appearance.

Their skins were chalky white from living mostly in darkness. Their eyes protruded from their heads, swollen by the excessive amounts of the elixir they swallowed daily as priestesses of Raik. A cold, stale draft accompanied their movements.

They placed the trays on a table in front of the raven-haired woman and waited. Raikana lifted the figurine from around her neck and passed it over the platters.

"Raik, we partake of the bodies of our enemies in your honor," she intoned, then turned to the two women. "Serve the men first."

She watched with quiet satisfaction as the commanders reluctantly lifted pieces of roasted meat and forced themselves to eat.

One of them, a newly recruited mercenary officer, turned pale and leaned over his chair, emptying the contents of his stomach on the floor.

Raikana glanced at him and clapped her hands together.

Two guards appeared. She pointed to the quivering officer. The guards moved to his side and helped him to his feet.

"I am all right now," he said, but the guards ignored his words. They dragged him from the room. As they reached the doorway, the young commander tried to break free.

"I meant no harm, your Majesty. I was just fatigued," he cried out.

"Then you must rest," she replied emotionlessly.

The others in the temple remained still. Each knew they would never see the officer again. Not alive.

Raikana gestured to the two priestesses to remove the platters, then resumed the conversation as if nothing had happened.

"The lord of Kalabria must be killed or captured before the Sjarik is over."

The magician had helped her put together a timetable for conquering this country. Next they were to cross the mountains and capture the fabled cities beyond them, but the stubborn Kalabrians were interfering with her plans.

"We should wait until after the Sjarik," Captain Lomark, a tall man with a ringlet of brown hair that framed his otherwise bald head, suggested timidly. "It will give us time to prepare new warriors, your Majesty."

Her voice suddenly became high-pitched and icy. "No. We will do it now!"

The most senior of her commanders, a tall ox of a man named Vaka, rose angrily to his feet.

"Where will we get enough warriors to overrun this accursed country?"

She smiled at him coldly. "The magician will get us more."

Raikana turned away from them dismissively. Yes, she thought, the magician could do what she wanted from him. She allowed no one to speak his name, but now she murmured it to herself reassuringly. Nis, the great Nis, was here to help her fulfill her destiny.

THE GUARD KEPT HAMMERING at the door that led to the magician's sanctum. No one answered.

He started to leave and return the tiny canister to the queen, then remembered her temper and knelt down.

Carefully he leaned it against the door, then stood up and quickly moved down the corridor.

THE MAGICIAN SAT in a chair and ignored the banging. The energy was leaving him too rapidly. He was facing the one opponent he could not best—time. There was no way to measure exactly how much longer the essential energy would last before existence ceased.

Preliminary exploration of this world indicated there were limited deposits of the glowing stones. Soon he would complete the depopulation of the region around them so they could be safely explored.

His tests had indicated potentially large supplies of the rare energy rocks on the other world. But there were large populations to eliminate before they could be properly investigated.

He had searched a thousand worlds before he finally found signs of the stones on two. The agents he had sent out to locate them had been unsuccessful.

But he couldn't conduct a personal search until the target areas had been made safe. Meantime he would have to husband what energy he had left.

After all, he was the last of the Guardians. His destiny had been determined when time began. He had to bring logic and order to all of the worlds. And to achieve this, he must destroy everything and everyone who did not conform.

8

The American and the slight monk walked side by side down the narrow stone corridor of the temple. Mutt and Jeff in Cambodia, Hogan thought as he flashed an amused look at Mok Seng, who didn't respond.

Hogan was tall and broad. Every exposed part of his body displayed well-trained muscles. By contrast, the monk next to him was barely five feet tall. He gave the appearance of a man who had been fed a less-than-subsistence diet for many years.

Hogan knew how misleading the monk's appearance was. Inside the frail body was a lifetime of wisdom and disciplined skills. A master of the Cambodian version of kung-fu and kick-boxing, the smaller man used the strength of his enemies to defeat them.

When they began the long walk, Hogan had sensed a danger, but it had faded before he was certain. Perhaps he had only imagined something was wrong. Just the way he imagined Brom and his strange world. He hoped so.

Mok Seng stopped in front of a wooden door and opened it. Waiting invitingly before them was a large room, its floor a vast stretch of hardwood. It was the practice room.

"I still can't imagine who would want a snake put in my room," Hogan said, pausing in the corridor.

Mok Seng stretched up to tap the American's head with a thin finger.

"You spend too much time worrying why you do not have all the answers to your questions."

Hogan shrugged. He felt his concern had been summarily dismissed, and wasn't in the mood for one of the monk's lectures. "Are we here to talk or to practice?"

Mok Seng moved to the center of the room and waited.

"To do both," the monk replied. He gestured for Hogan to join him. Reluctantly the American moved closer to the frail-looking man and bowed his head in respect.

Mok Seng studied him. "Shall we work with the sword?"

Hogan remembered his recent dream in which he had decapitated a berserk attacker. "I think I've had enough practice with the sword for now."

The monk nodded. "Then we shall help you remember the right way." He pulled himself erect. "Repeat the first of the Four Noble Truths of Buddha," he ordered.

"Existence inevitably leads to unhappiness," Hogan answered, prudently backing away from the monk. Too many times his teacher had sneaked in a kick or throw while lecturing him.

"You do not trust me," the monk commented. "I am trying to teach you the rules for living a serene life." Then he moved swiftly and tossed the larger man to the floor with a simple leg throw and thrust of an outstretched arm.

Hogan fell backward but turned and hit the hardwood floor with his side. He glared up at the monk.

"Is this the serene life you have in mind?"

"I was illustrating the first truth. *Now* you are unhappy."

The large man glared at the wizened monk. "You're in the wrong business," Hogan commented bitterly. "You ought to take up martial arts as a profession."

"That is not a proper profession for a holy man of peace," the small Cambodian replied calmly.

The elderly monk moved back a few steps and got into a fighting position. His feet were slightly apart, weight centered between them so he could shift in any direction. His arms were somewhat bent and held before him, callused palms ready to counteract any aggressive moves.

"You could have fooled me," the American snapped.

Quickly he struggled to his feet. Raising his hands in front of himself like a wary heavyweight boxer, Hogan waited for an opening.

"That is not a proper position," the frail holy man pointed out.

"Like you said, little grandfather, I'm only a barbarian. I don't know what is proper," the American muttered.

The monk sighed and lowered his hands. "What is the second Noble Truth?"

"Unhappiness is caused by desire." Hogan clamped down hard on his teeth and launched a flying kick that threw the small monk to the floor.

When the man didn't stir, Hogan became worried. Perhaps he'd hit him too hard.

At last Mok Seng opened his eyes and studied Hogan. "Now we know why you are unhappy. You desire to kill me."

Hogan held out his hand. Mok Seng gripped it and stood up, then spun around and launched a series of palm and elbow blows, ending with a kick-boxing blow to the American's chin.

Hogan collapsed from the sudden assault. A thousand demons jabbed spears into his body. His eyes were filled with the blinding light of pain. He rolled over and lay on his stomach.

Above him he heard the thin voice of the elderly holy man. "What is the third Noble Truth?"

The kick to the chin had clamped Hogan's teeth on his tongue. It was difficult to speak.

"The third Noble Truth," the monk insisted.

Hogan ran his bleeding tongue across his teeth. They were all there. "Unhappiness can be avoided by the crushing of desire," he mumbled.

He pushed himself up from the floor. The monk moved back and shook his head as he watched Hogan getting up.

"Six years I have tried to teach you how to think and still you learn nothing."

Hogan rubbed his sides gently. The stabbing pain was beginning to subside to a dull throbbing. "Most opponents don't expect me to recite something while we're fighting," Hogan growled.

The monk ignored the criticism. "What is the fourth Noble Truth?"

Hogan gave up. Nothing he said bothered the small monk.

"Desire can be crushed by following the moral path that leads to the ultimate reality and eternal serenity."

The Cambodian pointed a frail finger at him. "You still question your dreams?"

The question surprised Hogan. Was the meaning of his dreams about to be explained?

"Yes."

"You cannot find eternal serenity until you accept them without question."

Hogan started to protest, then stopped. What was the point?

The aged monk watched the American's face betray his inner reactions and smiled. "Come. It is time to teach you the heart thrust."

As usual the holy man had surprised him again. "What the hell is a heart thrust?"

Mok Seng sat on the floor and crossed his legs in the lotus position. He gestured for Hogan to join him. As he eased down into a crossed-legged posture, Hogan regretted asking the question. Now he would be forced to listen to one of Mok Seng's anecdotes.

"Many years ago a frail old monk traveled alone through a land. He was stopped by a strong young man, surrounded by many friends, who told him he must pay a toll to pass on the road.

"The elderly holy man complained that he had traveled this same road many times in the past without paying a toll.

"'That was before I took it over,' the young bully said. 'Because you are old, I will give you a choice. You can either pay me or fight me.'

"The monk decided that since he had no money and had to continue his journey to reach a certain temple, his only choice was to fight. The bully promised not to hurt the frail monk too much and commenced to use his superior knowledge of hand and foot fighting to attack the old man.

"Each time the monk was knocked down by a blow, he rose to his feet and waited for the bully to hit him again. Finally the young man stopped and looked at the monk in disgust. 'You haven't even tried to defend yourself. If you do not do so, I shall be forced to kill you.'

"Looking sad, the frail old man agreed to fight back. Again the young man attacked him. But this time the elderly man cupped the fingers of his right hand and forced them into the area below the young bully's heart.

"The young man laughed at him. 'That is it? That is what you call fighting back?' His friends, who had watched the one-sided battle, joined him in the mocking laughter.

"Suddenly the young bully stopped laughing and fell to the ground. His friends rushed over and knelt to help their friend. But he was beyond help. He was dead."

"And the blow he used was the 'heart thrust.'"

The monk nodded and stood up. He signaled Hogan to stand. The American sat still and stared into space.

Mok Seng smiled at him. "You are thinking that the young man and the elderly monk are much like us?"

Hogan shook his head. "No. I was just wondering what kind of sick mind would use a snake as a weapon."

The abbot looked annoyed. "Be grateful for the gift you have received," he said sternly.

Surprised at the comment, Hogan looked up. A deadly snake had almost injected its fatal venom in him, so what was there to be grateful about? he thought. He didn't mask his sarcasm. "Grateful?"

"Now you know your enemies wish to stop your journey, so you can be prepared."

He held an extremely thin hand out to Hogan. "Come. It is time for me to demonstrate the heart thrust."

Hogan ignored the offered hand and jumped to his feet. His jaw and sides still ached. "I'm not sure I'm ready for this."

"Come. I will be very gentle with you," Mok Seng said with a benign smile.

Hogan stared at him skeptically as he reluctantly moved back into the center of the room.

9

His powerful body was motionless as Black Jack Hogan watched the wet, grassy field from the cover of the stand of hardwood trees. The helicopter was late. It should have picked him up an hour ago. Even if it had arrived on time, he would have been barely able to make the international flight to Washington.

Getting him to Washington was Wilson's problem. Hogan was more concerned with his surroundings at the moment. He was certain someone was waiting behind a tree for the opportunity to kill him. And he was unarmed.

It would have been difficult to try to smuggle his jungle knife or his Beretta aboard the international flight. He would have to rely on instinct and the martial arts he had mastered.

The powerfully built man carefully peered into the jungle that surrounded him and listened for sounds of an enemy.

The dense growth was alive with the noises of living creatures, the soft rustlings of small animals moving through the thick undergrowth and the call of the birds. The staccato pinging of large drops of rain, just beginning their four-month-long siege of the land, provided the subtle rhythm of drums for the jungle symphony.

A profusion of trees, shrubs, wildflowers and exotic plants competed with one another for space in the thickly populated wilderness. Bright, almost electrified colors from the different growing things vied for Hogan's attention.

The rain started to come down faster. Hogan was just about to open his suitcase and take out his thin, olive green raincoat when he remembered he had a ready source of rain coverings at hand.

He looked around for a vine of elephant ears. The huge-leafed plant grew everywhere. Cambodian farmers wore the leaves as makeshift raincoats during the monsoon season.

There was one behind him. He tore two leaves from the vine and draped them across his broad shoulders.

As he continued his wait for the helicopter from Bangkok, Hogan looked around and knew one reason he'd agreed to make the trip. The rainy season was starting. Four months of heavy rainfall. Even the monks, always smiling and at peace with life, would become irritable by the end of the third month.

If there was ever a good time to leave Angkor Wat, this was it.

When he heard the quiet voice speaking precise English, he wasn't startled. It was the gentleness that succeeded in not setting off his inner alarms.

"Come back," it said.

Hogan turned. It was Mok Seng, looking small and lost in the greenery except for the absurdly large golf umbrella over his head. His expression was stern.

"You will come back." It was an order, not a request.

"Yes," Hogan promised.

"You are starting to become a good student. Perhaps you are ready to learn now."

Moving closer, Mok Seng handed him a small brass amulet strung on a length of tanned leather. "Wear this for guidance from Buddha," he murmured, then turned and disappeared back into the jungle.

Hogan took out the raincoat from his carry-on bag and spread it on the ground. Then he sat down on it and studied the antique metal cylinder. Inside, he knew, were Buddhist prayers for his safety and spiritual well-being. Well, it wouldn't hurt, he thought. He'd need whatever help he could get—from any source. He slipped the leather necklace over his head then leaned his head against a tree, closed his eyes and waited for the helicopter to arrive.

He saw a shimmering cloud under his eyelids, an enticing play of light....

BROM HAD BEEN DOZING when he felt the hands removing his bandages. He lifted his head and smiled at the bull-like man in the white robe. Panka was the high priest and head physician of Kalabria and was responsible for the more than five hundred priest-healers and temple virgins under him.

Brom had never understood the need for so many attendants. At one time, five hundred years ago, the virgins were there to be sacrificed to the gods in time of drought or pestilence. But sacrifices had been outlawed by one of his ancestors.

He'd once asked Mondlock why virgins were still needed, especially since so many of them no longer had the qualities that went with the position's requirements. Namely, many of them had lovers—or they could have, if they wanted.

But Mondlock merely said that after all, everything needed a name, and dismissed the issue.

"Mondlock said you needed a physician," the white-robed healer said.

There was no warmth in the older man's voice, and Brom looked at him curiously. Panka had been his best friend as a child, worried over every scratch. And later, when he had grown up, fussing about every battle wound. Certainly he had heard by now about Brom's injuries, yet he seemed unconcerned.

Brom tried to make a joke. "Since you're head of the priests and temple virgins, I wanted your advice."

This had always been Panka's signal to smile expectantly. Instead, he remained expressionless.

"I was thinking of changing the title of the temple virgins," Brom continued, not bothering to hide his grin.

"What do you think of the idea of calling them temple wives?"

The elderly bald priest stared at him. "But they are not married, Lord Brom."

Brom tried to laugh, but he was too weak to do so. "Then get them married before we breed a country full of temple bastards."

Without a word the bald man knelt beside the exhausted warrior and cleansed the wounds with lotions from the healing bag tendered to him by the two priests who had accompanied him.

"Not even a small joke to take my mind off the pain, Panka?"

Panka changed the subject. "You have lost much blood. You will need to drink two cups of the blood of a bull to help replace it."

Brom shuddered at the harshness of the recommended cure, and surrendered himself to the hands of the healer.

Grim faced, the bald man expertly covered his wounds with a dark, reddish ointment that stung like the fang of a serpent.

Carefully folding a fresh pad, Panka laid it over the treated area and finally wrapped a length of clean cloth around Brom's head and fastened it with the sticky residue from a kador tree.

With great effort Brom lifted his head and looked at the still-silent healer. He was puzzled by the man's unusual behavior.

"Is something wrong, Panka?"

"No, Lord. I have been grieving for those who died." Bending his head and obscuring his eyes from Brom's gaze, he ran his hands over the warrior's back. "I will treat your back," the bald man announced.

As Brom surrendered to his ministrations, he began to wonder if weakness was truly overtaking his mind and making his eyes go dim. In a corner of the tent, he saw a shimmering cloud, and within it, he fancied he could discern the dark features of a man. With a resigned groan, Brom closed his eyes for a minute to chase the vision away.

Brom could feel the warm hands kneading his neck muscles. Slowly he felt the thick knots of tension melt as Panka's hands seduced each frozen muscle into relaxing.

Brom's eyes began to close. He felt the hands slip down to his shoulders to unlock the knotted mass of well-developed muscles, then the hands withdrew.

A vaguely familiar voice shouted a warning. "Watch out!"

The Kalabrian thought he must have entered a strange vision of his own making when, from a corner of his eye, he saw the god of vengeance charge toward him. Turning his head, he saw the healer's hand raised above him, grasping a short, twisted knife. Panka's face was twisted in hate, but he seemed to be looking through, rather than at Brom.

As weak as he was, the red-haired warrior was able to twist his body out of the path of the knife.

When Panka's jagged weapon descended, it ripped open one of the large cushions. Feathers flew in every direction.

The next second the intruder tackled him, tumbling both of them onto the ground.

The two priests who'd accompanied the high priest pulled out daggers from under their robes and rushed the fighter who had appeared from nowhere.

Letting go of the fallen man, he rolled over and jumped to his feet. Expertly the strange-looking warrior slashed the point of a booted foot and crunched the thin bones in a knife-wielding priest's wrist. As the stunned man stared at his suddenly limp hand, the warrior snatched up the fallen knife and rammed it into the robed man's left eye. Blood and gelatinous tissue oozed out of the empty socket as the priest sank to the carpeted ground.

Enraged, his companion threw himself at the transparent-eyed avenger, slashing at him with the knife in his hands.

Almost calmly the new arrival expertly sidestepped the attack and whipped the edge of the blade across the priest's throat, exposing his windpipe and esophagus. Gurgling blood, the priest fell on top of the other robed body.

Panka had been diverted by the battle between his priests and the strange figure who had magically appeared. Now he turned his attention back to the red-haired figure on the cushions, gripping his knife with both hands for the killing blow.

Ignoring the wrenching pain caused by movement, Brom grabbed the krall at his side and forced every ounce of his energy into his right arm. With an anger-driven thrust, he rammed it up into the midsection of the assassin, slicing open the abdomen.

Blood and bits of tissue and intestines gushed down on him. Panka dropped to the ground heavily, and a crimson stain quickly spread around his body.

Stunned by the unexpected attack, Brom stared at the still form on the ground in shock.

His weak voice was filled with confusion. "Why, Panka?"

Slowly the eyes of the mortally wounded man opened. They were already glazed. "You...you are the enemy of my god. It is my duty to destroy you."

As Brom watched in stunned immobility, the hands of the dying man desperately felt around for the fallen knife. His fingers touched the edge of the weapon and struggled to wrap themselves around it.

Sobbing for the loss of a friend, Brom lifted the krall and swiftly severed the arterial vessel in the wounded man's neck. He fell back against the cushions, then lifted his eyes to thank the god of vengeance.

He was gone. Only the hint of a shimmering cloud remained in the tent.

Exhausted, the Kalabrian leader was enveloped by a welcome darkness.

SEVERAL HOURS LATER Brom awakened to the sensation of warm water gently washing his face and body. He opened his eyes. Lovely Mora was looking down at him with an expression of concern.

He smiled weakly at her and touched her face with a hand, as though to confirm that he was really awake. Then he looked around and saw that Panka's body was gone.

Mora saw the confusion in Brom's expression. "Mondlock had the body removed," she hastened to inform him.

Brom's face was filled with sadness. "Panka helped raise me from before I could take a step by myself."

A new voice spoke from behind Mora. Brom recognized it as Mondlock's. The Knower moved closer and held up a metal necklace. The grayish metal figurine of the monstrous demon god hung from it.

"He was wearing this under his robes. So were the other two. They were converts to Raik."

So many had converted to Raik in the past year that Brom had insisted each of his warriors be inspected regularly to make sure they weren't wearing one of the accursed necklaces. He hadn't thought it necessary to extend the order to the priests.

"You exhausted yourself killing all three," Mondlock warned. "Now you must rest."

Mora studied the red-bearded face. "Shall I bring you some gruel?"

Brom found some strength at last. "No! Bring me meat and something strong and nourishing to drink, woman."

"Bring him a cup of ox blood," Mondlock ordered.

"And something to kill its taste," Brom added.

Mora looked at Mondlock, who nodded approvingly. She bowed her head and left the spacious tent.

Brom stared at the tent opening for a long time. Mondlock seemed to read his mind. "She is quiet and gentle. You couldn't choose a better woman for a mate."

The Kalabrian leader wondered how the wise man would describe the dance warrior if he had ever witnessed their lovemaking—playful and ferocious by turns. Certainly not gentle.

"She will when the time comes," he agreed, then changed the subject. "The Manhood Tests will be run during the Sjarik. It is important that our men maintain their courage. I will lead them."

Even if it kills me, he told himself silently.

10

The room was grand in scale, even though it was Saddam's private study. Oil paintings of his heroes adorned the walls—former ruthless but decisive rulers of Mesopotamia—and the marble floor was strewn with Persian rugs of rich hue. Antique weapons—swords from Damascus and pistols inlaid with mother-of-pearl—were displayed in glass cases as mute witness to his military ambitions.

Saddam stared at the map above his desk. Yes, he had plans for his country, and beyond that, for this turmoil-torn part of the world. He had come to unify his brethren, and if it had to be accomplished with steel and blood and fire, then so be it. The means justified the end, he thought, and it was a glorious end. He was tired of being a helpless bystander while superpowers shaped the destiny of his people. He was taking matters into his own hands.

He glanced at his watch and frowned. In only a few minutes Dr. Nis would be before him to allay his uncertainty over the newest plans that were supposed to go a long way to assure his victory. And the man better offer some certainty, Saddam thought darkly. He was a man of action who believed in the sword, the cannon, the fireball of modern destruction. This new drug was an unknown factor...something he wasn't used to dealing with. It tampered with men's minds, but who knew just what was there? Maybe, besides the devils, an angel or two could be unlocked....

His brooding was interrupted when an aide knocked and ushered in Dr. Nis. Saddam waved the blond scientist over to a chair facing his desk and leaned forward expectantly.

"Are you sure we know what we are getting into? How can we control these people when they ingest the drug? I am not used to such dealings.... You know I like to strike directly, get to the heart of the matter, rather than rely on indirect and questionable methods. We are talking about war, not some decadent Western approach!"

Nis smoothed down his hair with a faintly fatigued expression and darted Saddam a look from his unfathomable Oriental eyes. He rearranged his elegant and beautiful form in the chair before he answered.

"You saw the results yourself at the Yazidi festival. Actually, we do not need to be able to do anything beyond feeding the drug to unsuspecting populations. No triggering device, such as the silver whistle, is needed, because all on its own the drug induces a psychosis driven by submerged killing instincts. When needed, we can also implant specific suggestions in the minds of people, suggestions that will be liberated and acted upon once they ingest the substance. Remember, all men have the devil in them."

Saddam looked uncomfortable. "But what if ... some angel is also freed? And our plans will go in the opposite direction? Or if these people will simply kill themselves in isolation?"

"There are no angels in the depths of men's souls. It all goes back to raw primordial life ... to brute nature. At any rate, the drug is designed to appeal to suppressed base instincts, and anybody who has ever been denied his desire, or had been hurt in any way, or cast aside, treated unfairly by life or a fellow worker or playmate ... will remember that magnified in a thousand ways and will be ready to strike out in revenge.... It's very simple, really."

"You know what will happen to you if this doesn't work?" Saddam asked icily. "I brook no failures."

"I am at the service of your greater plans. The world is in sore need of ... ah ... order. And the drug has been refined, so we do not need to do anything other than administer it, and when appropriate, implant some suggestions in select people's mind for a more specific aim. Trust me—I'm no ordinary scientist.''

With that, Nis stood, bowed slightly in Saddam's direction and left the study. He took care to close the door softly behind him, and strolled along the spacious corridor.

Inside he was smiling at Saddam's antics. The man's far-reaching plans, indeed! He, Nis, was called upon to do two things: sustain his being, and create order in all the far-flung orders of the universe. Nothing could stand in the way. What was taking place here was nothing more than the merest grain of sand in the eternal hourglass, in circular time. Saddam was a tool who would unwittingly assist him in his search for the precious substance that would allow him to realize his destiny.

On a long stretch of empty hallway he stood deep in thought, and the next second he had vanished....

BLACK JACK HOGAN popped open his eyes and stared at the baby-faced officer leaning out of the Bell AH-1 Huey Cobra.

Shaking his head to clear his mind, he realized he must have fallen asleep and had another of his nightmares.

He got up and rolled up his raincoat. Shoving it into his suitcase, he looked more closely at the smooth-faced pilot inside the helicopter. He appeared young enough to be a college student, not a military officer.

Aside from his appearance, it was not the Bangkok-based pilot who usually picked him up.

''Where's Tim Hawkins?''

''Off for thirty days' leave to Tokyo. I'm Ed Rankin.'' He touched the bars on his opened shirt collar. ''Captain, like Hawkins. Sorry I'm late. Weather wasn't too good in Bangkok.'' He looked at the controls, then eyed Hogan again as he remembered something. ''Mr. Lancaster said he'd meet you at customs with your ticket.''

"Did he call you?"

"Naw. Showed up at the field." He grinned again. "Funny looking little guy, isn't he?"

Hogan climbed into the helicopter. He considered taking the seat next to the pilot, then decided he preferred being alone rather than being subjected to chatter, and slid into one of the two seats behind the air jockey.

As the pilot manipulated the Huey above the dense Cambodian jungle, Hogan could feel the weight of the rain-drenched air pressing down on his broad shoulders. He looked down at the small bag between his feet. It was good he'd decided to pack several extra shirts. The Air Force captain glanced down at the thick carpet of trees five hundred feet below them, then turned and stared at his passenger for a second before turning his full attention back to the controls.

Hogan shrugged and leaned back in his seat. The young captain seemed dull and harmless.

He let his mind wander through the maze of questions he had. How many alternatives had Wilson investigated before contacting him? A lot, he suspected. He was always the last option.

He hated going to Washington. Washington was where the chess players lived. They sat around their huge desks and moved the pieces on the boards, sacrificing pawns while they went on with their fat, comfortable lives.

Washington was also where Evelyn was waiting for him. Hogan wondered how much of a coincidence it was that it was she who'd brought the evidence about Saddam to Wilson. It was beginning to feel like a scenario Wilson would create.

If anybody should be familiar with Wilson's complex plots, he should. They'd worked together for too many years, starting when he was a counterinsurgency specialist based in Thailand and Wilson was an Intelligence field officer there.

After the squad he'd led on a secret mission into Cambodia had been annihilated, he'd managed to survive by pretending to be dead.

The monks at the small temple near Angkok Wat had found him. "You'd been more in Buddha's company than in ours," the small Cambodian monk who ran the temple later told him.

For six months he lived with them, until he was strong enough to return to the United States. Then he spent another year in Walter Reed Hospital, fighting the daily nightmares of slain friends. Wilson, the courtly government Intelligence expert who had conceived the Cambodian mission, had visited him regularly.

Finally Hogan had been discharged from the hospital. And from the Army, as being unfit for active duty.

There was nowhere to go. No family, no friends, no place he really belonged. He had returned to a world in which he was an outsider.

Wilson had urged him to return to the temple in northwestern Cambodia, near the ruins of Angkor Wat, and try to find peace there. Hogan could still remember the words of his last visit.

"As far as this country is concerned, the missions you've been on—especially the Cambodian mission—never happened."

Wilson had contacted him a few months later to meet him in Bangkok. During that meeting he had told Hogan an order for his death had been issued.

Hogan remembered how stunned he'd been at the news, how cheated and betrayed he'd felt. At that point Wilson offered a possible solution. He was going to need someone with practical field experience to carry out a variety of missions without asking a lot of questions. Somebody with brains and enough savvy to understand the world and the issues at stake—and to act like a seasoned warrior when the need arose.

The job wasn't in the true sphere of spying, as Wilson himself was no longer exclusively in that domain. His business card, with the Presidential seal embossed in gold, said he was a special assistant to the President of the United States.

When Hogan established that he didn't need to be based in Washington, they came to an agreement.

That had been six years ago, and he'd lived here ever since.

Hogan leaned his head out of the helicopter. He could see the tops of the spiral towers of the Angkor Wat ruins thrusting proudly above the trees, and in the distance he heard a soft sound of a deep-throated gong summoning the monks to their midday vegetarian meal.

The helicopter pilot's words brought him out of his private thoughts.

"We've got some mechanical difficulties. I'm going to have to set down and radio for help."

Hogan looked out his window. Through the misty rain, he could see the endless green stretches below. He wondered what the trouble was—or if there really was trouble.

"Exactly what's wrong?"

"I'm not sure," the pilot replied hurriedly. "But I'm radioing for another helicopter." He pointed to the ground seven hundred feet below. "I gave them our location."

He turned and stared down at the rain-drenched ground. There was a small clearing set in the middle of the jungle.

The moment the helicopter touched the water-soaked tall grass, Hogan started out the door. He had no intention of sitting exposed in the middle of a field.

He was heading for the thick forests across the field when he heard the pilot's voice. "Hold it!"

Turning around, Hogan saw the Colt Commander .45 ACP in the young captain's hand. Puzzled, he stopped and stared at the pilot's face.

The man looked angry. But Hogan saw something else. Fear.

"Are you supposed to kill me?"

"No, just keep you here. Get your hands up."

Hogan raised his hands above his head. "Keep me here for what?"

"Until the others arrive."

"Why?"

"Mister, I just follow orders."

Hogan saw that the hand holding the gun was shaking. He swept his eyes around for something he could use as a weapon.

Something was moving through the tall grass. At first he thought it was a small animal, then he saw the multicolored body of a three-foot-long krait trying to escape the light steady drizzle.

The deadly serpents were commonplace throughout India and Southeast Asia. Like many of the more potently venomous snakes, kraits were known for their usually placid temperaments.

An idea began to formulate in his mind, and he kept the pilot busy talking. "Why are they coming for me?"

"I'm not sure," the captain said hesitantly.

The snake had paused in its journey. Slowly Hogan edged closer to it.

"What am I supposed to have done?"

The pilot looked beyond Hogan, as though expecting to spot somebody behind him. Hogan wondered who was supposed to arrive. "Just shut up. I don't want to talk about it," Rankin shouted angrily.

"Why not? Are you ashamed of it?"

The captain's voice began to waver. "They didn't tell me." He forced the anger back into his tone. "But you know why."

A scant ten inches separated the snake from him. He glanced down. The angular head was raised as the reptile tested the air for vibrations. Hogan reviewed in his mind Mok Seng's technique with the venomous snake. Even if he was uncertain, he had no choice but to try it.

"I don't know. What did they tell you?"

All pretense of calm had been dropped by the pilot. His voice quavered as he replied. "They made it clear you were a traitor. You must have done something pretty terrible."

Hogan moved toward the snake an inch at a time. He didn't want the snake to strike in self-defense or slither out of reach.

"When are the others arriving?"

He could see the pilot searching the area with his eyes. "They were supposed to be waiting for us—for me."

As Hogan braced himself for the dive, he said, "Maybe they're not coming."

He saw that the pilot couldn't resist turning his head to search the area again. Swiftly he bent down and gripped the writhing snake behind its head. He could hear the pilot's answer, "They'll be here." Using both hands, Hogan pitched the snake at the suddenly terrified pilot and, while the young officer raised his hands to push the writhing missile away, dived for his legs.

The twisting serpent struck at the captain's face, injecting its venom into his left eye and cheek. Screaming, the hysterical officer dropped the handgun to tear the snake away from his face.

The snake fell to the ground and quickly slithered away while the screaming pilot kept tearing at his eye.

Hogan grabbed the fallen weapon, then jumped to his feet.

The pilot had collapsed. Writhing around in fear and pain, he started weeping.

There was nothing Hogan could do to help. He could see the shadow of numbness as the poison began to course through the young man's body.

Bending close, he asked, "Who ordered you to do this?"

The weeping had turned into moans and muffled prayers. Hogan put his ear close to the dying man's mouth, but there was no answer. Hogan looked at the suddenly rigid form. He knew the young captain would never have to answer another question until he arrived at the gates of wherever his final resting place was.

He closed the eyelids of the dead officer and started to get to his feet when he heard a blood-curdling battle scream.

11

Hogan saw black-clad men running toward him, shouting something in a Cambodian dialect. Recklessly they charged across the clearing, spraying a wall of lead in his direction from their AK-47s.

These were not trained fighters, or they would have held their fire until they were closer, where their rounds would not fall short of their target.

Quickly Hogan raced to the other side of the helicopter, but it was a poor shield. The thin metal was no protection against high-powered ammunition. But at least it provided him with temporary cover until he could calculate his next moves.

He looked behind him. There was too much open field to attempt a dash for the wooded area. He would have to make his stand here.

Quickly he checked the clip in the Colt. There were seven rounds. Not much defense against the six men with AK-47s.

Cautiously he raised his body so he could see the attackers through the open doors of the helicopter. They had stopped firing as they moved toward the aircraft.

Clad in the peasant clothes of guerrillas, they wore crude straw hats and elephant-ear leaves across their shoulders to protect them from the rain.

They looked young. Hogan stared at their savage expressions and knew he was in trouble. They were primed to kill.

Hogan waited for the two outer men to move around the rear of the helicopter. They'd be close enough for the Colt in his hand to be effective.

The first charged around the front in a burst of bravado, accompanied by loud incoherent shouting, and raised his assault rifle.

Hogan braced his automatic with both hands and fired twice. As Hogan had intended, the two shots tore a huge cavern in the attacker's chest. A fountain of blood from the cavity showered on the tall grass as the dead guerrilla fell forward.

Swiftly Hogan turned and saw the second attacker just as the gunman started squeezing the trigger of his deadly weapon. Hogan dived to the ground and rolled away, firing as he did.

His first shot carved a path through the enemy's side, and the second severed the large artery in the neck. Dropping his rifle, the wounded man pressed his hand against the wound and tried to keep the vital fluid from escaping.

Hogan fired twice more, this time at the black-clad guerrila's chest. Blood poured through the torn dark fabric and discolored him. The would-be assassin fell to the ground, while rain diluted the crimson flow and formed a thin red pool around the still body.

Hogan felt a burning in his left shoulder. He glanced at it. His perspiration-dampened cotton shirt had been torn by lead. A large red patch began to stain the light-colored fabric.

Quickly he slipped out of the sweat-soaked shirt and glanced at the two large holes in his shoulder.

He wondered if there was any lead embedded in his flesh, but there was no time to worry about it now. He could hear the shouts of the remaining four guerrillas on the other side of the helicopter.

He looked at his automatic. How many shots had he fired? Five, he thought. Only two rounds were left.

He dropped the Colt and scooped up the AK-47. There was a 30-round banana clip in it. Fighting off nausea and the growing desire to just close his eyes, Hogan crawled along the soggy ground and worked his way around the aircraft.

The four remaining men saw him at the same time. He turned his weapon on them, focusing his attention on the closest two.

The stunned attackers gasped as hot metal from Black Jack's weapon tore into their bodies.

Hogan was having trouble keeping his eyes open. The last two of the attackers glanced at one another triumphantly, then turned to the American and fired their weapons in a sweeping arc.

As Black Jack stared, he saw a shimmering in the air and out of it emerged a huge sword. Glistening as it carved the air, it severed the head from the body of one guerrilla in a single movement, then came down on the other and severed his gun arm.

Brom, the red-bearded warrior of his dreams, was holding it.

He looked weak and ill. Then Hogan saw the large red stain in the dream warrior's side. Almost as if one of the guerilla bullets had hit him.

Without a word the warrior pulled out his krall and rammed it into the chest of the armless guerrilla.

"The gods live in a strange world," he said, shaking his head as he looked around at the jungle that surrounded them. "Even the Forbidden Region is safer than living here."

Hogan stared at the ground. The severed head and arm that lay in the middle of a small puddle were no dream.

He looked back to where Brom had been standing. Nothing but tall grass and bushes were there now.

He heard groaning behind him. One of the fallen attackers was not dead. Stumbling toward him, Hogan aimed the borrowed AK-47 at the moving form and fired three rounds.

The bullets tore into the spine of the fallen figure, and the groaning stopped.

Would others come if these attackers didn't return? He couldn't wait to find out, not in his condition.

He'd have to make it out on foot. Reaching down, he searched the nearby body of a guerrilla. He grabbed several more banana clips for the AK-47 and shoved them into his pants pocket, then forced himself to stand up and promptly fainted.

BROM STARED at the sword lying next to him. Its cutting edge was crusted with a viscous layer of blood. Bits of flesh and bone clung to it.

What a strange place was the land of the gods. Filled with steaming woods and strangely clad creatures who shouted and threw bolts of lightning from their fire-sticks at Komar. And the huge rounded object that sat at the edge of the open field. Obviously it was a cage of some kind, but its doors were open and whatever was inside had escaped. What kind of wild creature needed a cage that large?

He had seen nothing gentle or beautiful. What a difficult life the gods led, he mused. It made him glad he was not one of them.

He turned his head to look at Mora. She was lying near him on the cushion, curled up like a sleek cat with her back to him.

He reached out and touched her to wake her and relate what he had just seen, then felt the searing pain in his left side as he started to turn. He looked at the source of the burning. Fresh blood was flowing from a ragged hole.

Mora had awakened a little and moved closer. "Sleep first," she whispered, looking at him for a moment. "Then when you have regained your strength..."

Suddenly she noticed the blood pouring from his body and jumped to her feet.

"You have been wounded," she gasped, and quickly tore off the bottom of her thin gown. She folded it into a pad and pressed it against the wound.

"Hold this. I'll summon Mondlock and a healer," she said, snatching up her robe to cover her body as she ran out of the tent.

Brom felt the burning in his side. He closed his eyes and let exhaustion take over. His body felt weaker than it had ever felt, as if something had climbed inside of him and sucked at the center of his spirit.

He was too muzzy headed to think anymore, then he heard Mondlock talking to him. "Did you see who did this to you?"

He couldn't answer. No sound came out of his mouth.

He heard Mondlock asking a question of someone else. "Was he here all the time?"

Brom opened his eyes and saw Mora's worried face. He wanted to tell her it was nothing, but he was having difficulty keeping his eyes open.

Mora replied, "He was when I went to sleep near him." She hesitated. "I thought I heard a strange sound, but didn't awaken. Then he was touching me and I saw the wound." She hesitated again. "What caused it?"

"I am not certain," Mondlock replied. "These bits of molten metal were embedded in the raw wound. And his sword is covered with blood."

Brom wanted to tell Mondlock about Komar and the strange world he had found himself in, but he suddenly was too tired to do anything but let the darkness swallow him again.

AS HE SAW the shimmering cloud around him fade, Hogan wasn't sure what had happened. One second he had been lying in a field, surrounded by seven dead bodies. The next he was standing outside a tent and it was night. He was still gripping the assault rifle he had grabbed from the Cambodian bandit.

He looked up at the sky and stared at the twin moons. He had to be back in the Kalabria of his dreams.

He must have passed out after the battle, Hogan decided, and entered another dream.

He was having trouble focusing his mind, and the pain from the bullet hole in his shoulder and the slashed hand still seared. He looked around the camp and saw the dying camp fires. In the distance was a large tent, with the glow of fire inside. Even where he stood, thousands of yards away, he could smell the stench of the dead.

Somber-looking men, their heads covered with long veils, came out of the tent in pairs, carrying still forms on wooden pallets between them. They moved quietly into the fields and placed the wooden platforms on one of many stacks of similar stretchers.

He was certain this was Brom's camp. Even without knowing the tradition of the people the red-haired warrior led, Black Jack instinctively knew these were the undertakers, preparing bodies for burning. Soon there would be weeping and silent bitterness.

Hogan wondered why his living dream, as he had come to think of it, had brought him here.

Then he saw a small, bald-headed man kneeling at the edge of a tent. He wore the robes of a priest. Hogan had seen such clothes before in previous dreams.

The man was wielding a long knife to slash the tanned leather of the tent. In his other hand he held a coarse cloth sack.

Hogan staggered toward him and the kneeling man sensed the presence of another person and whirled around.

Hogan started to ask about Brom, then saw the blank-looking eyes.

Swiftly the robed figure jumped to his feet and turned the blade on Hogan, slashing at his arm and cutting into his wrist. Blood spurted from the wound, and the automatic weapon Hogan carried fell to the ground.

Surprised at the unexpected attack, Hogan moved back. Still grasping the cloth sack, the priest dived at him and tried to drive his weapon into Hogan's bowels.

Hogan twisted his body to avoid the flashing knife and glanced at the fallen assault rifle, wondering if he could reach it in time.

He saw blood from the slashed wrist running down his fingers and onto the ground. He'd have to act quickly, before he was gutted with the scalpel-sharp weapon.

The American reached for his jungle knife, then remembered it was still in his room at the temple.

Strength was draining from his body fast as he struggled to avoid the priest's knife thrusts. Forcing himself to ignore the pain and bleeding, he decided to use one of Mok Seng's tricks.

Inhaling to relax his body, he let the priest pour all of his energy into the next thrust, then quickly leaned to one side and stuck a foot between his opponent's legs.

The man stumbled but regained his balance and spun around to face the stranger, then twisted his body and struck the surprised Hogan hard in the shoulder with the heavy handle of his weapon.

The carved metal dug into the fresh wound. Hogan grunted at the pain and fell to the ground. With a muttered curse the crazed man threw himself at him, and straddling Hogan's chest, the enraged priest raised the knife high as if he were about to perform a sacrificial ceremony. "Raik, I kill this man for you!"

Hogan took advantage of the moment and put his remaining strength into throwing the man from him. The surprised attacker fell to the ground and stared at Hogan for a moment, then tried to stab him again.

Hogan knew he was running out of strength. All he could do was let Mok Seng's training take over his body.

The furious priest jerked the knife above him for the death thrust. Hogan channeled whatever energy was left in him into his right hand, then wrapped his left around the blade and tried to push it away from him, feeling the edge bite into his palm.

Hogan knew if he made even a slight error, he was dead. Swiftly he thrust the fingers of his right hand against the priest's body. Searching desperately for exactly the right spot below the solar plexus, he felt the softness the monk had described, and forced his fingers to dig deep.

As Mok Seng had promised, he could feel the small path between the bony structure that protected the vital organs. But his fingers had almost stopped obeying his commands. He called on whatever adrenaline was left in him and shoved his fingers up to the priest's heart.

He remembered the abbot's instructions and kept striking his fingers against the pumping valve, feeling the heart working harder to fight back then finally weakening.

The priest dropped the knife and sack and tried to tear Hogan's penetrating fingers away, but the brawny man forced his bleeding hand against the robed man's throat and grabbed for his windpipe.

As if some demon inside was egging him on, the priest shouted a curse. "Raik will punish you."

Hogan didn't bother answering. He had been punished enough for one day.

Suddenly the priest's body shivered, then jerked toward the sky as a spasm raced through it.

The death scream that tore from the lips of the robed man was loud and pitiful as Hogan watched the veins in the priest's neck inflate and his face twist in fear and pain. He screamed one more time, then fell forward on top of the American's bleeding form in a violent death shiver.

Hogan tried to lift his body free of the other man's dead weight. He kept pushing his hands at the heavy form that had once been a man.

He glanced at the coarse sack on the ground and saw a slithering creature race out of it and rush into the darkness. Hogan hadn't seen it clearly, but would have sworn it had been a small snake.

He remembered the snake under his bed in the temple and wondered if there were any connection between the two just as his body finally shut down and he slumped into a coma.

12

Mora heard the screams first. The desperate shrieking of a man struggling not to die. She grabbed a dagger and jumped to her feet.

Brom opened his eyes. For a moment he had thought the pitiful shouts were part of a dream, then he saw her running toward the opening and reached for his krall.

He tried to stand, then fell back on the cushions.

"Mondlock came and dressed your new wounds while you slept. But he said you need rest," she said quickly, pulling a garment over her bare body. "I will see who screamed."

Mondlock entered before she could go outside. He saw the warrior staring at him, then at the bandage around his arm.

"I thought I dreamed you cleaned my wound and covered it."

"The wound in your arm had tiny bits of metal. Not all of them could be removed," he said.

"Never mind my wound. Who was screaming?"

"The new high priest, Masahlik."

Mora looked puzzled. "What happened?"

"We found him behind your tent, holding a krall. There was a slit in the animal skin."

"Was he stopping an assassin?"

Mondlock held up a necklace. The grayish metal figurine of Raik was suspended from it.

"This was around his neck. And there are other strange things. I searched the grounds around the tent, but could find no weapon that would have left slivers of metal in you."

Brom turned to Mora. "Hand him my sword."

But Mondlock stopped her with a gesture. "I saw the blood. Do you remember what happened?"

"I thought I had dreamed that I had saved Komar from his enemies." Brom looked at his bandaged arm. "It wasn't a dream. One of them fired a fire-stick and tore a hole in it."

"Ah, here comes your Uncle Draka," Mondlock remarked as a gray-bearded man swept into the tent.

Brom looked over expectantly. "How did the priest reach my tent without being stopped?"

"The two who guarded your tent let the priest pass, assuming you had summoned him, Lord Brom." He saw the look of disgust on Brom's face, and added, "Both of them have been put to death for their failure to protect you."

The red-haired warrior was about to voice a sharp retort when Mondlock stopped him. "What's done cannot be undone." He turned to the gray-bearded commander. "Does the man who killed the high priest still live?"

"Yes. Two of the priests are outside, trying to bind his wounds. He has lost much blood. He may not survive the night."

Mora sounded concerned. "He will certainly die in the chill." She turned and looked at Brom, staring at him expectantly.

"Yes," Brom agreed. "Bring him into my tent."

"The priests could take him to their tent and care for him there," Draka suggested. "He is a stranger, not one of us."

"He is a hero who has given his life to save mine. Bring him here."

Draka bowed his head. "As you wish," he said, then he and the Knower went outside to give orders, and shortly two guards entered the tent, carrying a wooden pallet. The still form's upper body was naked, and thick pads of blood-stained cloth covered his hands and shoulder.

Coming behind them were Mondlock and Draka.

Brom strained to see the man's face, then realized he was lying facedown.

"Turn him over," he insisted.

"Let him rest first, Lord Brom," Mondlock suggested.

"He can rest for as long as he needs after I gaze on the face of he who saved my life."

Draka interrupted. "I must arrange for new guards to protect your tent," he said, and left before anyone could stop him.

Reluctantly the Knower signaled the guards to carry out the request.

Mora watched from a distance as they did, then moved closer to gaze on the man's features.

Brom saw the shock on her face.

"What is it you see?"

Mora tried to speak, but words refused to come. Grabbing the howling sword, Brom used it as a crutch and pushed himself erect, then stumbled across to the wooden pallet.

He stared down at the face of the man who had saved his life.

The features of Komar stared back at him.

He turned to Mora, who shook her head in shocked disbelief, then looked at Mondlock for an explanation.

Mondlock's face was empty of expression.

"This was no god," Brom said, "but a man. Gods don't retain wounds and bleed. Who is he, Mondlock?"

"As you said, Lord Brom. A hero."

Mora looked confused. "Why would he masquerade as Komar?"

Brom felt the rage building like a roaring fire inside of him. "Must be a trick of Raik's. This is one of his spies!"

Mondlock leaned down and examined Hogan. "He wears no necklace of Raik."

But the Kalabrian leader would listen to no one. "Then he is a mercenary who has come here for some dishonorable reason."

Mondlock shook his head. There was no arguing with the huge man when he was this angry. He glanced at the straw-blond woman. Usually he could look to her for assistance in calming Brom. But her face was filled with fury.

Mondlock gestured for the two stunned guards to leave, and with looks of gratitude the pair of nervous soldiers rushed out of the tent.

"He has made fun of our gods," Brom bellowed. "And of me."

"He saved your life," the Knower reminded him.

"For some nefarious reason, no doubt. There is only one punishment to suit his crime."

Brom wrapped both hands around the howling sword that had served as a crutch.

Mora tried to stop him. "No, Brom. Let him live until he can explain his actions," she pleaded.

Blind rage stopped her words from having any effect. Stumbling over the sudden weight of the huge weapon, Brom tried to steady his uncertain legs as he raised the sword.

The room was fast becoming a confusion of blurry images.

Mora's face was cloudy. He could still hear her voice clearly. "If he must die, call the soldiers to do it."

Brom could feel the nausea rushing into his mouth. Still, the honor of Kalabria was at stake.

"To kill this man is to kill yourself," Mondlock warned sternly.

Brom tried to justify his action. "At least my honor will not be sullied." But the words had come out a jumble of sounds.

He managed to get the great sword over his head. His wrists were having difficulty holding the blade steady, and suddenly the howling sword weighed more than two soldiers. He stared at the face of the unconscious creature he had once considered his god, his friend.

Thoughts raced through his mind. He had been betrayed. Honor needed to be revenged.

He tried to blink the clouds from his eyes so he could separate the head from the body.

Then he fell forward and crashed to the ground, unconscious, still gripping the huge sword.

13

Hogan felt the soft, warm body next to him and turned his head. He beheld the slender girl next to him with astonishment. She was sound asleep, but her body was pressed against him. Through the thin gauze of her garment, he could feel her soft bosom nestled against his side.

He studied her face. It was pretty and small, like a child's, but her lips looked full and soft, like a woman's. He was tempted to kiss them.

But it was her hair that fascinated him most. He had never seen hair that looked more like the color of unripe strawberries than hers.

It was all very well to be lying next to such a delightful creature, but he had to find out where he was.

He let his eyes wander around the room.

He was in a large tent. Beneath him he could feel the hard wood. For a moment he thought he was back at the temple, then realized he wasn't. Mok Seng would never let someone who looked like the young girl next to him corrupt the serene thoughts of his monks.

He turned his head and saw the mass of red hair sprawled against thick cushions.

The red hair reminded him of Brom, and Hogan suddenly knew where he was. In Kalabria.

Back in his dreams.

He remembered the fight he dreamed of having with the priest, then looked down at his hands.

They were bandaged. A glance at his left shoulder, and he saw the thick pads of cloth that covered the bullet wound.

The wounds still hurt, but surprisingly less than they had last night.

Or was it a lot of nights ago?

He remembered being ambushed by the helicopter, and thought of the severed head and arm in the field.

If this wasn't a dream, there was another possibility. He had lost touch with reality and was condemned to the dream forever.

There was a strange, offensive odor in the tent. He wondered if it was coming from his body. He sniffed himself.

No, the smell was not his, and it wasn't coming from the girl next to him.

He looked around for the AK-47. It was gone.

The extra ammunition had been in his pants pockets.

His pants pockets?

He moved his hand under the thin cover draped over him. The coarse pants were gone. He was naked.

For a moment he panicked, then tried to sit up. The girl stirred and opened her eyes. Looking pleased that he was awake, she sat up and smiled at him.

"You are back with us. I must tell the Knower."

She started to stand. Hogan reached out a hand that barely obeyed him, but he managed to grab her wrist.

"No, wait. Talk to me first."

She looked unsure. "I was told to summon Mondlock the moment your eyes were opened."

"Where am I?"

She laughed quietly. "In Lord Brom's tent, of course."

"In Kalabria?"

She seemed amused by the question. "Where else would the lord have his tent?"

"Who are you?"

"Astrah. I am one of the temple virgins," she said. "I helped the priest-healers bind your wounds."

Hogan couldn't keep the disappointed look from his face. "Temple virgin?"

The girl smiled softly and added, "It is just a title."

Hogan sighed in relief, then remembered something. "How long have I been here?"

"You were brought in during the darkness."

Once again Hogan tried to sit up, but Astrah gently pushed him down.

"I've got to get going," Hogan protested. "Wilson will have my head if I don't show up."

She looked puzzled. "You spoke of this Wilson in your sleep. Is he your king?"

Hogan smiled at the notion. "Sometimes he thinks he's my god."

"A real god?"

"Only in his mind," Black Jack assured her.

There was a soft moaning from the cushions next to where he was lying. The strawberry-haired girl jumped to her feet.

"Lord Brom is awakening. I must get Mora and the Knower," she said hurriedly as she dashed out of the tent.

The strong, unpleasant odor still filled the tent. As he wondered where it came from, Hogan turned his head and saw the red-bearded man of his dreams struggling to open his eyes. But he looked very real as Hogan took in the tousled hair and the softening effect of sleep on the fierce face.

Brom tossed in his sleep, then let his eyelids open to a slit. For a moment he stared at the ceiling of the tent, then slowly turned his head—and saw Hogan.

He turned and tried to grab for his weapons. His hand would barely obey him. Finally it reached the place where he usually kept his krall and felt around for the long knife.

It was gone.

Hogan watched the frantic response, too weak to move.

"Somebody took my gun, too," he said in a harsh whisper. "And my pants," he added bitterly.

"Gun?"

Hogan wondered if anybody in this dream understood anything he said. "Gun," he repeated patiently. "Bang, bang."

"Fire-stick," the huge man next to him said, finally understanding.

"Yes, fire-stick." Hogan tried to turn on his side and groaned as a wave of pain raced through him.

"Gods do not get wounded," Brom said accusingly. "You are not Komar."

"I never said I was."

"You acted like a god."

"I wouldn't know how a god acts. Ours don't get into a lot of battles."

Brom studied him for a long time without speaking. Hogan wondered what he was thinking.

"You fought like a god."

"It was their asses or mine," Hogan replied.

The bearded man continued to stare, then admitted, "You are a noble warrior."

"Thanks. You're pretty good, too."

Something suddenly bothered Brom. "The fire-stick? Was that a gift from your gods?"

Hogan remembered the headlines about weapons violence and made a face. "Where I come from, anyone who wants one can get their hands on a fire-stick."

"Could I use one?"

"With a few lessons."

The Kalabrian grunted with satisfaction. "How are you called where you come from?"

"Hogan. John Hogan—some people also call me Black Jack."

"I am Brom."

"I know."

Brom looked puzzled again. "How did you get here?"

Hogan shrugged. "I don't know."

"Strange," Brom muttered. "Nor do I know how I got to where you were." He looked thoughtful. "This is the doing of the gods."

Hogan shook his head. "Well, let's just say I'm puzzled by it all."

The redheaded warrior lowered his head. "You saved my life again," he said weakly.

"You saved mine, too. Remember?"

Brom remembered. "Who were those creatures?"

"I don't know. But they certainly didn't want me alive."

Brom grinned. "So it seemed." He thought of something. "What was that strange structure near you?"

Hogan was puzzled at the question, then realized the object of interest must be the helicopter. "It's a machine we use for traveling. We have many different kinds of machines for traveling in my world."

Brom showed confusion on his face. "Don't you have horses?"

The thought of Wilson riding a horse to get from Washington to Bangkok started Hogan laughing. "Yes, we also have horses."

Brom stared at him curiously. "Mondlock will soon be here. He will ask the gods to relieve your strange illness."

Now the companion of his nightmares thought he was nuts. Hogan turned his head away and let his eyes close.

The strange smell awakened him.

Hogan turned his head to his tent mate. "What's that smell?"

Brom lifted his head and sniffed the air. "What smell?"

Hogan knew when he'd smelled the same kind of foul odor—when a Cambodian farmer had slain a pig to roast in his honor.

Hogan lowered his head and watched the red-haired giant turn toward him with closed eyes. The smell was stronger now. He sniffed around him. He leaned over and sniffed again.

It was coming from the warrior next to him.

Brom opened his eyes and realized the strange man was staring at him.

"It's you," Hogan said accusingly. "You're the one who stinks."

Brom sniffed himself. And looked puzzled.

"When was the last time you took a bath?"

"The last time I was presented to the gods. At the time of the Warming Festival." He worked out the time in his head. "Forty sunrises ago."

"You bathe once a month?"

Brom seemed offended. "Of course not. I bath after every festival—after I present my marks of courage." He pointed to several streaks on his chest. "These smears are made by the blood of the enemy I've slain since the last festival."

"How can you stand sleeping with yourself?"

Brom looked disappointed. "You fight like a noble warrior, but you don't sound like one."

Hogan looked around and wondered where he could find some place to take a bath.

He might be, as his red-bearded tent mate had called him, a "noble warrior," but he didn't intend to smell like one.

14

Hiram Wilson was livid. Hogan had been missing for three days, and the wreckage of the helicopter had only been found that day.

He rounded on Paul Robertson, the retired general who served as liaison between the White House and the military. "What kind of donkeys do you have over in Thailand?"

"Calm down," the tall, stiff man said quietly. "There was a lot of territory to cover. Besides, Hogan's body wasn't even there."

Leaning back in his large leather chair, Wilson opened a drawer and took out one of his cigars. As he lit it, he looked steadily at the former military officer. "This puts a big hole in our ability to move against Saddam."

"Hogan wasn't all that stable. With or without him, Saddam will be stopped," Robertson predicted.

The ringing phone interrupted their conversation, and the smartly dressed southerner answered it.

"Dr. Evelyn Thomas is calling," his secretary announced.

He wondered what he could tell the woman. He'd suggested she use up the vacation time she had coming by touring the country at government expense.

He picked up the phone. "Dr. Thomas, Jack Hogan has been delayed a little longer, I'm afraid. If you can't wait for him to arrive, I'll understand." He listened to her response, then said "Very well," and hung up. Turning to Robertson, he remarked, "At least I put her on hold for a while—without revealing a thing."

Paul Robertson nodded approvingly, then stood to leave. "We'll be on the lookout. In the meantime, I've got a flight to catch to New York City." At Wilson's mildly curious look, he hastened to add, "Oh, nothing major. Just have to reassure a banker. You know how easily nervous these types can get." He marched to the door and waved back at Wilson reassuringly before he vanished from the room.

EVELYN THOMAS STARED at the telephone after she finished talking to Hiram Wilson, then put another call through to Dr. Nis. But he already knew that Hogan was missing, and merely reminded her to maintain her "cure," to take the soothing medication he gave her.

Standing in front of the large, well-lit mirror in the hotel suite the American Intelligence officer had provided, she swallowed the potion Dr. Nis had given her in a glass of water, and checked her appearance. At almost forty, her face still had the fresh softness of a student's. Her pale blond hair hung straight down, touching her shoulders.

She looked just like the flower child who had wandered the streets of the Haight-Ashbury district of San Francisco more than twenty years ago.

The flower child who had wandered to Arizona's red-rock country to find something in which she could believe. And met Jack Hogan.

As she remembered, the half Apache, half Scot was her greatest failure. She had thought that with his Indian heritage, he would have had a greater appreciation for alternative religions. But when he made it clear that he didn't believe in what he had termed "mystical junk food," she left him.

She had been looking forward to seeing him again. But, as Dr. Nis often had told her, "we all have to make sacrifices to achieve the higher purpose."

Besides, Jack would have teased her about still wearing the pendant he had given her when they'd lived together. If only he knew how its meaning had changed since then.

As she fingered the circular pendant she wore around her neck, she knew that to the casual observer it looked like the peace symbol of the sixties. Only those involved knew the pendant was the Cross of Nero. A symbol of the Satanic Church, it pledged those who wore it to work for the defeat of Christianity.

She checked in her purse for the address and remembered that the ceremony started at eight. She looked at her wristwatch. She'd have to hurry if she didn't want to be late.

Already she could imagine the high priest in his black robes standing in front of the altar with the inverted pentagram painted on it, and starting to chant the nine Satanic statements.

"Satan represents vengeance instead of turning the other cheek...."

SITTING AT THE WINDOW TABLE of New York's exclusive Blades Club, Paul Robertson passed on the information about Black Jack Hogan's disappearance.

"Good," the slight, dapper banker commented. "He was getting to be a nuisance. I'm sure my partners will be pleased with the news."

The tall, lanky retired military officer nervously fingered his trimmed graying mustache. Randall Manderill was the chairman of the International American Industrial Bank and had been Robertson's financial mainstay since he'd left the military. The government didn't give much money to retired generals, and the token salary he received from the President was less than he needed to maintain the estate he had purchased in Virginia.

For years the banker had been slipping him cash rewards for confidential information on government plans that could possibly affect his bank. Since Manderill had become a partner in an international consortium of bankers, the rewards had become substantially larger. So large that a numbered bank account had been opened for him abroad.

"You will make a deposit to my...retirement fund?" Robertson smiled at how delicately he worded the question.

Manderill nodded appreciatively. "I'll tell our friend in Zurich to take care of it, Paul."

ONLY MOK SENG was not worried. As the Cambodian monk studied the ancient scrolls of the Tibetan *Book of the Dead,* he could sense that the American's spirit didn't need that guidance yet.

It was the same as when the peasants had brought the body of John Hogan to him after the Khmer Rouge had murdered the children. He could sense life where there should not have been life, and he'd used all the skills he had been taught in the remote temple in Tibet to restore the American to the living.

Somewhere John Hogan lived. Mok Seng wasn't sure where he was, but wherever it was, Hogan was strong and proud and as ready for a fight as ever.

15

Brom's tent had been turned into a banquet hall to honor the warrior Komar.

Serving women scurried around the uniformed men with offerings of food or to refill their cups with the strong blend of honey and fermented grain, which was a mainstay of Kalabrian evening meals.

For herself, Mora had prepared a small dish of fowl steamed with vegetables and grain.

One of the women staggered back into the tent carrying a huge platter of flat-bakes, the soft thin baked grain cake that accompanied all Kalabrian meals. As she struggled around the room, the men grabbed handfuls of the large circular breads to wipe up the spicy gravies of the evening meal.

Mora had grabbed several and handed them to Brom. The temple virgin had followed her lead, handing one of the two flat-bakes she had snatched to Hogan, then hesitating before she allowed herself to nibble daintily on the other.

With the recent attempt on Brom's life in mind, Mora took no chances. Somebody could have slipped a poison among the ingredients. She had insisted that portions of each of the dishes be served to the large guard animals. And only after they seemed unharmed by the meals did she permit the women to serve the dishes to the men.

"Raikana grows stronger every day," Brom observed as he swallowed a mouthful of flat-bakes. "She seems to be allied with evil spirits, and her mediator may be the magician who is always by her side." The other men nodded their unhappy agreement.

Mondlock continued to dip small spoonfuls of his small and modest meal into his mouth.

"Nothing is left to keep her from the mountains if we fall," one of the commanders commented.

Muttering and grumbling resonated through the tent.

In addition to Tana, Raikana and her Jaddueii had already conquered the neighboring kingdoms of Stulika and Calipon, as well as the hilly lands of Hazak, ruled by the barbarous dictator, Lompak, who boiled his enemies in huge caldrons rather than hang them. No one had ever been able to broach the borders of Hazak before Raikana. The Kalabrians had warred with Tarak off and on for many years, neither side gaining or losing land.

One of the younger officers, known for his humor, put on a mournful face to ask, "If she could conquer the savage Lompak, what chance do we gentle Kalabrians have?"

Laughter rolled through the tents. No one throughout history had ever considered the Kalabrians gentle.

"Lompak was hated by his own people," Mondlock reminded the men. "It was easy for the priestess-queen to convince them to allow her troops to slip past the borders."

Brom was annoyed. "That wasn't how it was in Kalabria. Everyone has lived in harmony for many years."

The other men mumbled their agreement.

"Not everyone. Your father—may the gods protect his powerful spirit—had enemies."

Brom had gotten angry. "Who?"

"Most of them are dead. But even in the most peaceful of kingdoms, there are those who dream of taking over the throne."

A muttering went around as everyone remembered the days of mourning, then after a respectful silence, the more ordinary joys of life took over.

The women looked flushed and happy, pleased to be together with their menfolk.

Mora sat beside Brom, while Astrah leaned close to Hogan, trying to ignore the stares of the men who were fascinated by the glowing light red tint of her pale hair. Hogan glanced at her and saw her turn red at the continued, deliberate stare of one man.

It was a large, thick-muscled warrior sitting some way from them, but his growled words carried easily over the din. "She needs a real man, not some finicky washed and prettied up servant of god."

"Your mouth is big," Hogan said, directing his words at the offender.

Astrah touched his hand. "Zhuzak is a good warrior, but he is a little drunk."

"Maybe it's time somebody taught him how to behave," Black Jack said from between gritted teeth.

"I heard that, *Dula*," the drunk commander yelled. "Would you like to try?"

Hogan turned to Brom. *"Dula?"*

"It means small boy," Brom explained in a low voice. "I warn you, Zhuzak is the wrestling champion of the army."

The drunken officer got to his feet, threw his krall to the ground, tore off his metal breastplate and staggered to where Hogan sat.

"Care to be my teacher, *Dula?"*

Hogan looked at him. He was larger than he'd imagined. A grizzly bear of a man. The American could see the well-developed muscles heaving beneath battle-scarred skin.

He glanced at Brom. The Kalabrian leader shrugged.

Hogan laid down the krall the Kalabrian leader had given him as a gift, stood and glanced down at his bare feet. He wished he'd worn his boots.

"I won't need much strength to put this old man on his ass."

Zhuzak exploded in rage and wrapped his thick arms around Hogan's chest and tried to crush his ribs. Hogan felt the air rush out of his lungs. Whatever wrestling rules he had known back home didn't seem to apply here.

Struggling to free himself, he could feel blood rushing into his face. He started gasping for air as he tried every trick he had learned in the gymnasiums he used to haunt.

Elbow jabs and kicks had no effect. The Kalabrian wrestler kept squeezing tighter.

"In Kalabria a bout is declared ended when one of the opponents surrenders or dies," the Kalabrian growled in his ear.

The room had become a blur. Brom and Mora and Astrah were vague images, and the shouts of encouragement to the Kalabrian officer were like a death knell that irritated Hogan. Even if he had to die, he was determined not to surrender.

Desperately he tried a tactic he despised. Letting his head slump down to his chest, he wriggled his body as if he were trying to squirm free.

"Don't let him die, Zhuzak," someone shouted. "He was sent by the gods."

"Then they can have him back!" the wrestler shouted back.

As Hogan expected, the other man pulled him higher. Waiting until the arms around him started to squeeze him again, he snapped his head back with every ounce of energy he could find within himself.

When the back of his head rammed into Zhuzak's nose and mouth, he heard the gratifying cracking of facial bones.

The arms opened and Hogan fell to the ground. Jumping up, he turned and faced his bear of an opponent. The officer's face was a thick mask of blood.

The voices in the tent gasped, then shouted angrily at the newcomer in their midst.

Hogan could see the hate and fury in the man's eyes. It was no longer a wrestling match. It had became a death duel.

Zhuzak rushed at him, his massive fists clenched. He jerked his right arm back and swung. With a dancelike hop to the right, the American stepped out of his path and let the Kalabrian stumble into a group of onlookers, who quickly shoved him back on his feet. Turning, he spit blood at the ground as he waved a fist in the air.

"Are you going to dance instead of fight?"

The crowd cheered at the angry question. Shouts of "fight, fight, fight" echoed from every corner of the tent.

Hogan ignored the taunts and waited, balancing himself on the balls of his bare feet.

The Kalabrian wrestler stared back at him, then suddenly reached down and tore the krall from the scabbard of one of the officers.

"No!" the crowd shouted in disappointment.

Hogan heard Brom's sharp call and half turned just in time to catch the krall that came flying through the air.

In possession of a weapon at least, Black Jack watched the enraged man and made a decision. He tossed the knife at the ground near Brom's feet, where it struck point-first, quivering in the soft carpeting.

"I won't need a knife to teach this ox manners," he said loudly.

He could hear the crowd murmuring with approval. Now they were coming over to his side.

Zhuzak ignored the jeers of his fellows as he grasped the handle of the weapon and moved against his despised opponent, slashing the empty air as a warning of what was to come.

Hogan relaxed his body. If the Kalabrian followed form, he would twist his body and try to slice Hogan's stomach open. He waited until the other man came close to him.

As he expected, the huge man spun his body around and attacked with a vicious slice. Except the American wasn't at that spot anymore.

Hogan had danced out of the path of the knife.

Zhuzak's move had brought him face-to-face with his opponent. He started to pull his weapon back.

Hogan twisted in a turn, pushing his left foot between the wrestler's legs, then jerked his foot up against the testicles of the Kalabrian.

The crowd roared with laughter as the giant officer fell to his knees and dropped his weapon so he could grab himself with both hands.

Even as Hogan stood back to let the man recover a little, Zhuzak snatched the knife up and threw himself into attack.

Barefooted, the American kick-boxed the weapon from the wrestler's hand with a full-powered thrust to the soft side of his wrist. As the knife fell, the still-drunk officer got to his feet and started throwing punches at the empty air.

Hogan decided it was time to end the game. He whirled and delivered a smashing reverse roundhouse kick with the heel of his left foot, then followed it by hammering the practice-hardened edge of his right hand behind Zhuzak's ear.

With a soft gasp the huge wrestler collapsed on the ground like a suddenly emptied air bag.

Fuzzy from the wrestling bout, Hogan let Astrah lead him back to his place next to Brom as several soldiers carried the unconscious wrestler from the tent. After murmurings around the tent, a chorus of cheers went up for the strange warrior—a welcome from the Kalabrian fighting force.

16

The town of Carramah sat on the southwest rim of the aboriginal reserve two hundred miles from Darwin. Technically it wasn't really a town, more a place where miners and their families could shop for supplies, lift a chilled bottle of Foster's Lager, place a telephone call or get to exchange gossip.

Even in the brutal heat of early fall, several dozen men and women dressed in jeans and work shirts could be seen strolling along the lone street, occasionally dragging a hot and crabby youngster behind them.

But not today. Today the streets were empty of life except for the flying insects that hovered over the badly mutilated bodies of men, women and children sprawled on the street.

The windows of the sun-bleached wooden structures that contained the general store, the pub and the tiny telephone office had been smashed. So had the people, doors and everything else that was breakable inside.

Carramah looked as if some giant creature had suddenly charged into the hamlet intent on destroying everything that stood in his way, and had left behind him a microcosm of hell.

The distant sky carried a whisper of life as the almost inaudible sound of a small plane came closer.

Carramah had been the closest thing to a bustling community in the reserve since the discovery of uranium ore. Mining the radioactive mineral had been an important industry for the region, since it employed a large number of aborigines, for whom it was one of the very few sources of livelihood open to them—aside from government assistance. For many of them, the hamlet was a link to the outside world.

Then yesterday all of that ended.

Yesterday a large number of aborigines began to wander on foot toward the town. Each carried a spear, a rifle or both. Not unusual, since an important source of food was the wild game they killed.

Dressed in thin shirts and lightweight pants, the aborigines' concession to civilization, their numbers grew as others joined in the trek toward Carramah.

There was an aimlessness about their journey. Not as in a walkabout, where a man seeks to reconnect with his origins. This was more like the blind following a familiar path that they could not see.

Slowly they progressed, inching their way to Carramah, seemingly in no hurry to get there. Eventually their numbers had grown to several hundred.

In the rear a surplus army jeep moved slowly in back of them, maintaining a distance of about a hundred yards. Behind the wheel a grim-faced man in rancher clothes kept the vehicle moving at the pace of the walkers.

In the seat behind him was the remainder of the shipment he had received by cargo jet the previous day. Medical supplies from Qatir Chemicals. In less than a week, this land would be his to rule, and all because he agreed that when he took over, he would let them search the barren land for some stupid rocks.

"It's a good deal, mate," he told his wife beside him.

In a while the outline of the town buildings shimmered in the midday heat. Suddenly, as if the sight of the town had pressed a button in their heads, the trekkers began to be infused by an electrified energy.

Rushing forward, they charged at the handful of people on the streets, shouting incoherently as they swarmed around them and randomly slaughtered them.

Spreading out, the berserk attackers tore into every building to search for more victims. From inside, the screams of those who had been found pierced the fall air.

"Worked like a bloody charm," the jeep driver said into the phone when all was done.

SADDAM STORMED into Dr. Nis's office and demanded his attention.

"The manager of the plant informs me you have withdrawn vials of TX-133 and had them shipped by plane." He reached into his pocket and took out some of the vials, then shoved them into Nis's face. "You are here to assist me, not conduct some personal business on the side."

The more important Saddam felt, the more tiresome he got, Nis decided as he hung up the phone.

"I had altered the formula slightly. It was important to test it before you sent your agents across the border with it."

"That was dangerous. What if someone had discovered it?"

"The important thing is," the blond man replied in a tired voice, "that it worked even better than the original."

The colonel rubbed his hands together and smiled.

"Excellent. Then I can set the date for our mission." He started to leave the scientist's office, then stopped and stared at the blond man's drained expression.

"Are you feeling well?"

"Nothing that won't be corrected shortly," the man with the Oriental features replied softly.

17

Hogan shook his head. He could still not grasp, nor believe, what Mondlock had just told him and Brom. Not that the Knower had said very much, but the gist of it touched on those particular realms of the supernatural that Hogan could not profess to believe in. Somehow, because both Hogan and Brom had actually died and their spirits had wandered on, they had met up with each other and become linked in spirit, acquiring even each other's language skills, or so Mondlock had hinted. How all this had resulted in both of them coming back to their own worlds and then being connected to each other in some way, especially in times of need and danger, no one could explain. It was a mystery, Mondlock said, like all important and sacred things. Hah, Hogan snorted to himself, just like the kinds of things children are taught in Sunday school. But he could not deny that there had to have been an unusual turn of events rising above the general rules of physical life and death. After all, he had died, then had returned to his ordinary world of the living, but now here he was in another world in God-knew-what dimension of the universe, and all he knew was that he was not dreaming. . . .

No. These people were real, as was the stuff around him—the tables, the chairs, the tent. He heard the singing with his own ears, just the way he could hear the beating of the blood in his veins. And the people singing and drinking around him were real: he had seen them bleed, had seen their flesh torn in battle. But he had to chase the thoughts away. Such things were for Mondlock to think about, and for Mok Seng, Hogan amended mentally as he lifted his cup and glanced around the tent. He could see the nods of approval as the crowds continued to shout.

He sipped the cup of honeybrew Astrah had handed him and wondered if he should stand up and take a bow.

The question was answered when he realized the name they were calling was not his.

"Mora. Mora. Mora."

Black Jack looked at the straw-blond woman next to Brom. They wanted her.

Brom tried to stop her, but she got to her feet and smiled sweetly at the fire-topped warrior. "It is time to dance for you, Lord Brom." Then she gracefully left the tent before he could voice his objection.

Soon three musicians entered the huge room, sat cross-legged on one side of the tent and began to play. Then Mora returned, leading two excited steeds. Quickly the crowds moved back to give her room to perform.

Hogan stared at the spectacle in awe. Mora had changed into a dancer's costume. The tightly fitting blouse and pants covered her entire body, yet revealed so much. As she paraded the two animals around the center of the tent, her pointed nipples poked at the shiny fabric that tried to crush them. She swept her long arms, hidden inside flowing sleeves, in a dramatic gesture, then pointed a commanding finger at the musicians.

The rhythm of the music changed from a lighthearted to a challenging beat.

Mora's pace quickened as she continued to move in a circle. The soft, sensual pants she wore seemed painted on her slim, powerful body. As each part of her moved, so did the light, glittering fabric.

One by one she flirted with the men, teasing one with her smile and another with an outstretched hand she quickly pulled back when he reached to grab it.

The overamorous commander fell on his face to the laughter of his companions. As he moved back into place, he smilingly acknowledged defeat, then looked down at his waist.

The krall he wore in his belt was gone. Now Mora held it high.

She danced past Black Jack and Astrah, smiling at them, then continued to move seductively until she reached Brom's side and knelt before him.

He reached out a hand to grab her. Instead, she slipped on ' his lap, gently touched his face, then jumped back to her feet and triumphantly displayed the krall she had stolen from him.

"The Lady Mora is a thief," Brom shouted gleefully.

"But so beautiful you must forgive her, Lord," one of the commanders yelled back.

The room exploded into applause.

Mora held the two eighteen-inch knives above her head, then turned and ran toward the two nervously prancing mounts. With a single leap, she did a somersault in midair and landed with one foot on the back of each of the animals.

Again applause filled the air.

The music stopped. Only the drummer continued in a constant pattern that kept building.

"Watch," Astrah whispered excitedly to the American, squeezing his hand. Hogan was curious about what was to happen next.

He didn't have to wait long to find out.

Holding a krall in each outstretched hand, she jumped from horse to horse, then suddenly did a somersault, slashing the knives beneath her as she did, then landed on the backs of the animals again without a wasted motion.

The men cheered as the drumming slowed.

Then silence. Now was the time for the Kiss of the Kralls. Brom became tense. So did the others. All of them had seen skilled dancers cut apart on the razor-sharp edges during this final dance, cruelly killed by a mistimed move.

The straw-blond woman began the intricate pattern of turns and somersaults that would end with her pressing the sharpened tips of the two kralls against her throat as she dived from the mounts to the ground headfirst and, at the last minute, twisted into a final somersault to land on her feet and hold the kralls above her head.

The drummer kept pace with her moves.

First slow. Then the pace increased. Faster, faster, faster. The razor-sharp knives slashing a hair's width away from her unblemished skin with each turn.

The challenge was to see how close she could brandish the weapons without drawing blood. The self-mutilation of a dancer was frequent in the Kiss of the Kralls. Death was not unknown.

Brom gripped the edge of his cushion. Mondlock shook his head at the cruel spectacle. Only Mora seemed calm, twisting her slim form, leaping from back to back as she pressed the knives against her lips, her eyes, her neck, her chest. Then, throwing herself into the air and revolving rapidly, she landed on her feet on the backs of the nervous animals.

Then the final movement.

The drums stopped. Tension filled the room as Mora closed her eyes and moved into position.

Brom wanted to order her to stop. But he knew he couldn't. It would disgrace both of them.

Mora opened her eyes and smiled at him as if she understood how he felt.

She forced her eyes away from his. She went inside herself, and the eyes became glazed.

Then she looked down as if the ground didn't exist.

And threw her body at it.

Pressing the two knives against the sides of her neck, she let her body roll forward, then jumped into the air and landed on her feet.

Unmarked.

As the men stood and cheered her, Hogan glanced at the gray expression on Brom's face.

"That is quite a handful of woman you've got there," he commented.

Brom nodded, then glanced at the temple girl with Hogan.

"And you."

Astrah blushed while Hogan nodded his agreement.

18

When Hogan went to his tent with Astrah after the festivities, he told her gently that he would soon have to leave.

"This is not my home," he explained.

"It could be if you wanted. Lord Brom is like your brother, and the warriors admire you."

He shook his head, not knowing what else to say.

"At least wait until the Sjarik is over."

"Sjarik?"

She told him about the initiation rites—the Manhood Tests, as she called them. "Only women, old men and little children do not participate."

"There will be other Sjariks."

"You will be missed."

Hogan smiled nervously. He knew where she was heading. He decided to help her get there.

"By whom?"

"By Lord Brom and Mora and Mondlock the Knower."

"And you?"

Astrah lowered her eyes. She felt confused. When she thought Hogan was a god, she could get emotional about him, knowing it was an impossible dream. Now he was a man like other men. She corrected her words. *Not* like other men. But still a man.

And he would leave her, no matter how she felt. No, she decided, this was just as impossible as when he was a god.

She had meant to tell him that, but the words that came out of her mouth said something else. "I will never miss a man as I will miss you."

She felt him staring at her, then raised her head and looked back. His eyes were very clear, so she could see deep inside him. What she saw was the spirit of a great warrior and the heart of a good man, a man she could love.

Without speaking, she moved to his cushions and felt his arms close around her. For a moment she was afraid. Then, under his gentle movements, the fear disappeared and was replaced by feelings she had never experienced before.

The pain was slight and it was overwhelmed by the wondrous sensations that stirred up emotions she couldn't have imagined an hour earlier. Slowly at first, then more anxiously, they came together as he gently brought her to the ecstatic conviction that they were one and the same body.

"Now you shall always be with me," she whispered before she fell into a deep, joyous sleep in his arms.

As sleep started to claim him, Hogan saw a shimmering behind his eyelids. . . .

THE HASTILY CALLED conference was held at a small Swiss estate that had once housed a monastery. The bankers gathered around a long ornate table in what had been the large dining hall.

They had come from around the major cities of the world: London, Tokyo, New York City, Johannesburg and New Delhi.

Hans Zeibart wanted them to hear the status of their joint investment, the chemical plant in Qatir.

"First of all, it seems the American government's special agent has vanished."

Knowing smiles were exchanged around the table.

Zeibart held up his hand to maintain their attention.

"Second, Colonel Saddam is now ready to distribute the chemical."

"About time," the elegantly dressed Englishman commented, and several of the men at the table applauded.

"The colonel estimates that he should be ready to move his troops into the neighboring countries within thirty days."

The banker from Tokyo made a note on a small pad, then looked up at the speaker. "How long before we can open offices in them?"

Before the Swiss banker could answer, the Afrikaner from Johannesburg jumped in with another question. "How about distributing the chemical to other parts of the world?"

Randall Manderill, the American from New York, laughed. "You got a head start on the rest of the world with that test in Namibia."

"There are lot of other places down my way that need the chemical," the South African banker retorted in his Dutch-English accent.

"That is up to Colonel Saddam and Dr. Nis," Zeibart said, interrupting the debate. "The one thing both of them promised me when they called was that protecting our investment was their first priority."

The bankers gave the two absent men a long round of applause.

IN THE MORNING Black Jack Hogan woke up and found himself in a clearing. Looking around, he saw the familiar thick jungle that surrounded him and heard the sounds of life going on in their depths.

He was back in Cambodia in the middle of the rain in the same field where he'd been attacked.

So had he been dreaming? he asked himself. The question was answered when he looked at his clothing. The shirt and pants Astrah had brought him. And the bare feet.

He glanced at the object next to him. It was the ornately decorated knife sheathed in its metal scabbard that the red-bearded warrior had given him.

Brom's wise man must have been right about one thing. It still didn't make sense, but he believed he wouldn't have to wait until there was danger to be with Brom ... or with Astrah.

He smiled as he remembered last night with her. The fragrance of her newly found passion still clung to his body.

Looking around for his guns, he remembered he had left them with the Kalabrian leader. At least, he comforted himself, Brom seemed to understand how they worked.

Then Hiram Wilson and Operation Fuse Point came to mind. By now the man in Washington had probably torn the world apart searching for him. He decided he'd better find a way to get there before Wilson started sending agents to the moon.

The sound of tinkling bells penetrated the babble of jungle noises. Hogan recognized the sound. A farmer was leading an animal-drawn wagon along a dirt trail. He raced in the direction of the bells.

As he ran, he tried to remember how to say, "Please take me to the temple in Angkor Wat," in Cambodian.

MOK SENG was expressionless as he handed the farmer a number of coins. Then, after they went through the ritual of parting, he turned to the large American.

"So you have decided to honor us again."

There was a hard edge to the small Cambodian's voice. Hogan started to explain what had happened, but Mok Seng held up a hand.

"Please do not. I have already been given more versions than this elderly mind can absorb."

Hogan was curious. "From whom?"

"The *pnong* Wilson in Washington has been intruding on the serenity of this peaceful place daily with calls inquiring if we have heard anything about you." He sniffed, offended. "As if we should care whether or not you bothered living."

Hogan wanted to smile but restrained himself. Now he knew the monk had been worried.

"Anybody else?"

"A rude American military officer named Wallace from the Thai city to the north flew down here with six uniformed men and insisted on searching the temple personally. I would have asked him to leave, but to honor your memory I permitted him to look for himself."

The monk glanced at the long knife the American was carrying. "A gift?"

Hogan nodded. "I guess I better call Wilson before he calls again." He turned to go to his room.

"There was someone else."

He stopped and turned to look at a suddenly solemn face. "Who?"

"Not who, but what. There was an alien presence that invaded these walls. It stayed for a brief moment, then disappeared. But while it was here, it was obviously seeking evidence of you."

There had been a time when Hogan would have laughed at the superstitious-sounding words. But, after what he had experienced, he believed Mok Seng.

The monk changed his tone. "Now, go on, call this Wilson before he decides to fly here on one of his large, offensive birds and totally destroy our peaceful existence," he directed sternly, sounding like a schoolmaster.

AT FIRST Hiram Wilson thought somebody was playing a tasteless joke on him.

He put his hand over the mouthpiece of the phone and said so to Paul Robertson, who'd been making the rounds in Washington.

"Some clown is pretending to be Jack Hogan."

After a few minutes of conversation, he was certain it was Black Jack who was calling.

"Hold on," Wilson said into the phone, and turned to his visitor. "If you don't want to hear a southern gentleman swear like a horse thief, you'll leave my office."

Paul Robertson took the hint and walked out. He had an urgent call to make. To a banker in New York City.

Wilson let his pent-up emotions pour into the phone. "Where the hell have you been? We found the helicopter and the seven dead bodies, but you weren't there."

Black Jack had planned an explanation. "A farmer found me and took me to his village. I must have been unconscious for a few days."

"A few days?" Wilson exploded again. "You've been missing for almost two weeks."

"The last time something like this happened, I was out for almost a month," the voice from Cambodia reminded him.

Wilson quieted down. He'd forgotten about last year.

"I'll send a helicopter to fly you to Bangkok."

"No." Black Jack Hogan's voice had a hard edge to it. "I'll get there on my own."

"Nervous about helicopters, Jack?" The question had a bite in it.

"Only the ones you send to pick me up."

Wilson winced. Hogan had bitten back.

19

The wizened man in filthy rags shouted loudly. "I've found it!"

Disgusted, the hard-bitten sergeant pretended he didn't hear him.

In the past three days the four Jaddueii had proclaimed that they'd discovered the strange rocks, just because the figurines they wore around their necks had changed color.

The magician had warned him that all that meant was the presence of energy matter, not necessarily the specific rocks for which he was searching. And each time Kepok went to inspect their findings, what they were holding was a piece of melted silicon that reflected the sunlight or some colored stones.

"Sure, sure," Kepok grumbled. He was tempted to ignore the old man, then decided he would humor him. There wasn't much else to do in this scorching wasteland.

Except watch for the dragons who were supposed to inhabit the Forbidden Region.

As a professional soldier, Kepok had fought for many strange rulers. But none as strange as the queen and her magician. Still, they paid well and he had an ample supply of drink and women at his disposal.

Kneeling beside the grinning face, he studied the desert ground but saw nothing. He was about to stand up when the elderly man asked, "Don't you see it?"

Kepok saw nothing. "There is nothing here but sand."

The small man continued to point at the ground. "It's right there."

Kepok looked closely at where the long, bony finger was aimed. There was something there. A tiny speck that glowed.

He had expected something larger. Still, something was better than nothing. There was the final test the magician had told him to use.

"Pick it up," he ordered.

Smiling triumphantly, the old man scooped his hand under the sand and lifted it up. As the grains of sand slid from his opened palm, Kepok could see the glowing particle more clearly.

Suddenly the wizened Jaddueii began to whimper as the glowing bit of rock burned a hole in his hand.

Quickly the grizzled sergeant shoved the metal-lined bag the magician had given him under the upraised hand and waited until the rock burned through flesh and bone and fell into it.

"Back," he shouted to the other three in the party, and moved quickly to his horse.

The old man fell to the sand and started screaming in pain. Ignoring him and the other three, Kepok kicked his animal into a gallop and raced for the palace where the queen and the magician were waiting.

There would be a reward from the magician for this discovery. Lots to drink, women—and perhaps a promotion to captain.

Then he could tell that sick bastard, Vaka, to whom he reported, to take out his hangover-induced anger on somebody else.

KEPOK KNOCKED at the door of the magician's inner sanctum. This time he wasn't nervous or worried. The door opened and the magician looked out. The sergeant was surprised at how thin and ill he looked.

He told him of his find.

"Let me see it," the magician insisted, opening the door wide.

Kepok entered and looked around. The large room was empty.

He wondered where the others were. He'd heard that the magician had a lot of workers helping him concoct the strange elixir that kept the Jaddueii under control.

It wasn't any of his business. His business was fighting.

Kepok handed him the metal-lined bag.

"No. Spill the contents on the floor."

The magician seemed pleased as he stared at the tiny speck that glistened on the stones.

He turned to the sergeant. "The queen will reward you. Go."

Kepok had expected something more. A compliment for his discovery, perhaps.

The magician kept staring at the glistening particle, then gave a severe, reprimanding look to the armored man.

Quickly Kepok left the room.

Now that he was alone, the magician focused his thoughts on the tiny object. He could feel the energy from it pouring into him. His strength was beginning to return.

Not enough, but more than he'd had a few minutes ago.

There was enough for at least six months, he calculated. More than enough time to find additional supplies of the life-sustaining stones.

He had to live. He was the last of the Guardians, the oldest of all the races in every dimension. They were the finest of those who were created, pure energy, and not just energy, but that rarest of energy that carries with it the gift of intelligence. The Guardians were not meant to measure life span; they were to live forever.

But something had gone wrong, and now he was the last of his kind. If he could find more of the glowing stones—the very essence of his particular life-form—then he could renew himself, and from there, influence all the dimensions and all their worlds, and his name would become sacred.

20

Khalid peered out of the bedroom window of his apartment and checked to see if there was anyone watching him. As usual the streets of Qatir were deserted in the midday sun.

This was the day he would depart from this land of the insane. He had had enough of Saddam and his mad dreams. And of the strange scientist who worked for him.

The Americans should be grateful that he was risking his life to tell them of the mad adventure the colonel was about to begin—and pay him well for the information.

Quickly he shoved the last stack of American hundred-dollar bills into his large leather briefcase, then checked to make sure he hadn't forgotten the vials or the whistle.

He looked at himself in the full-length mirror in his bedroom. The ivory-colored slacks and bright turquoise silk shirt made him look like a tourist.

Better that than a soldier on the run.

The price of capture was a slow, painful death. Saddam never forgave, and Khalid knew that soon the enraged colonel would send troops to search for him.

Khalid patted the leather bag. The ten thousand dollars in it would buy him a wardrobe with which to start a new life someplace in South America.

There was a deserted hut in the mountains where he could hide for a few days, until Saddam's men gave up looking for him. Then he would make his way to the perfect place to leave the country. Just beyond where the Yazidis had their shrine. The more superstitious border guards refused to serve near the habitations of the devil worshipers.

After he had crossed the border and was safely on his way to someplace like Rio, the Americans would send in their agent to do whatever he wanted to Saddam and his death factory.

THE SWISS BANKER had called to pass along the news that the American agent, Hogan, was on his way to Washington. The information had been passed up through the secret communications chain, from the retired general in the White House to the banker in New York and then to Zurich.

Saddam walked into the scientist's office in the chemical plant to tell him.

"I called you a few minutes ago after the banker's call," the uniformed colonel said, "but you weren't here."

"I went to check on the energy," Nis explained.

The colonel studied the scientist's face. "Well, whatever was wrong with you seems to have cleared up."

Nis changed the subject. "What are your plans for the American agent?"

Saddam eased down into a chair in front of the desk and tapped his lips with his fingers.

"I have made arrangements to take care of him before he leaves the United States."

He tugged at the sleeve of his uniform angrily. No one was to interfere with his plans, especially not some insignificant American agent. He had already disposed of four of their spies. He couldn't understand why getting rid of this one was taking so much time.

Very soon he would send the team Nis had trained over the borders to contaminate the water supplies with the drug. His troops poised to move, Saddam would wait for the populations to destroy one another before moving in.

Dr. Nis asked something he didn't fully understand. Showing his annoyance at the interference in his thinking, Saddam stared at him. "What was your question?"

"I asked what will you do if the arrangements are as unsuccessful as the others have been?"

Saddam weighed the question for a few minutes.

"There are other agents I could hire to conclude this matter," he said. "But since we are only weeks away from moving across the borders, it would not be wise to arouse too much attention."

Clearing his throat delicately, the colonel continued, "*If* the men I've hired fail, I have decided to let the American doctor get rid of this man Hogan."

Now Saddam was taking credit for his idea.

"An excellent idea. I'll alert her," Nis replied.

"Good. Now I have to see what happened to Khalid. He seems to be missing," Saddam announced as he hauled himself out of the chair.

Dr. Nis delayed placing his call until the uniformed man had left, then while he waited for his secretary to announce that the doctor was on the line, Nis wondered how the media would treat the story if she had to be the instrument of Hogan's elimination.

A likely scenario was that the more scandal-oriented publications would focus on a resurrected relationship that had failed, resulting in a murder-suicide carried out by the erratic female physician. When they investigated her strange fascinations, not even the more skeptical would question that there was any other motive, or anybody else involved.

Then his plans could proceed with no further interruption.

21

"Please fasten your seat belts in preparation for landing."

Hogan heard the mechanical-sounding woman's voice over the speaker system and opened his eyes.

Fastening his seat belt, he cast a brief glance out of his window. It was dusk. Night would soon be here. Through the haze, he could see the outlines of Washington, D.C.

The nonstop flight from San Francisco had been the last of a series of long flights, and he was tired. A stop at the car rental stand, the quick meeting with Wilson, then a hot bath and a night's sleep at a hotel would solve his immediate problems.

Except for who was trying to kill him, and why.

There had been a moment in San Francisco when he thought he was being followed. Either it had been his imagination, or the tailer was an expert.

It didn't matter. No one could get to him up here.

Except with a missile.

Evelyn and he were to meet in the morning. He didn't waste time wondering how she would look or how he would feel seeing her again after all these years. Those questions would be answered tomorrow.

He looked out the window again.

And saw the reflection of a shimmering cloud in it.

Stunned, he turned quickly to the empty seat beside him, only it wasn't empty any longer.

The red-bearded Kalabrian was sitting in it, looking terrified and clutching in his hands his sword and the AK-47 Hogan had left behind. As usual, his krall was in his waistband.

Black Jack had brought the krall Brom had given him. But it was safely stored in the bag he'd checked in, away from the electronic inspection of airport X-ray machines.

Hogan looked around to see if any of the other passengers had seen Brom, then got up and grabbed two blankets from the rack overhead. Wrapping them around the sword, knife and assault rifle, he slipped the weapons under the seat and whispered, "What are you doing here?"

Brom looked around the cabin. "What kind of creature are we in?"

"It's not a creature. It's called a jet plane, like a big bird, you know."

The warrior glanced out of the small window, then pulled back quickly. Nervously he turned to the American.

"What keeps it up in the air?"

"I'll explain another time. You haven't told me why you're here."

Gripping the arms of his seat tightly, Brom closed his eyes. "I was gathering my equipment for the Sjarik. The Sjarik is . . ." he started to explain.

"Astrah told me what the Sjarik is," Black Jack snapped impatiently. "Go on."

"We leave on the sunrise for the Manhood Tests," the bearded man continued, still keeping his eyes tightly shut. "Suddenly I had this sense that you were in trouble. So I gathered my weapons, and the shimmering cloud appeared and seemed to swallow me."

He opened his eyes and looked around again.

"And here I am." He didn't look pleased. "Wherever here is."

Hogan leaned back in his seat. What kind of trouble had Brom sensed? He trusted the Kalabrian's intuition. He just wished he knew when it was going to happen.

He moved his foot under the seat and felt the blanket-wrapped weapons. At least this time he would be armed.

"We're landing in a place called Washington," he said. "It's the capital of my country."

The bearded man nodded. "Like Tella is—was—until the sick usurper invaded it."

Hogan examined his companion and wondered how the denizens of Washington would react to his appearance.

Brom was wearing a loose, shirtlike top, and wide-legged pants of some thin material. With his long hair and beard he looked like a throwback to the hippie days of the sixties. Actually, Hogan mused, like someone Evelyn would have dated back then.

Given the way most people dressed these days, the Kalabrian wouldn't be noticed enough to cause a problem. He stood out all right, with his fierce face and carriage, but if he kept his sword and krall out of sight, he could pass for just another strange personage in a world that was spawning them by the thousands.

Hogan's prediction proved correct. Except for the cabin attendant who stared at them when Brom and Hogan left the plane, carrying the blanket-wrapped weapons, everybody ignored them after giving them a somewhat surprised second glance.

Even the car rental agent, who asked if Brom would be one of the drivers, looked surprised when Black Jack said no.

The bearded Kalabrian's reaction to riding in a car amused the American. After the car drove off, Brom attempted to open the door and jump out, but finally he calmed down and studied the interior.

"Is this what you use in your world instead of horses?"

Hogan nodded as he concentrated on keeping up with the traffic. Maneuvering across the Arlington Memorial Bridge during evening rush hour wasn't easy at the best of times.

Brom stared out of his window, fascinated by the ornate buildings and the crowds of cars trying to force their way across the span over the Potomac River.

"Is this where your people live?"

"In and around Washington. We have lots of other cities that are even bigger."

Brom glanced up at some of the tall buildings they were passing.

"I feel like I'm in the middle of a giant box built of stone. Where is the open land and the clean air you said you missed?"

Black Jack smiled wryly. "That's why I won't live here."

"A wise decision." The Kalabrian stared at the statue of Abraham Lincoln, well lit at night for the tourists. He pointed to it. "Is that one of your gods?"

"No. One of our great leaders."

Brom nodded with understanding. "In my world there are also countries where the leaders have statues of themselves built." He reached down to the floor and unwrapped the weapons, then stared at the world outside the rental car.

"Is this the danger I sensed?"

"Maybe," Hogan replied. "But this is only what everyone faces each day." But something told him he was wrong. There was another danger. He glanced in his rearview mirror at the large dark brown luxury car that had followed him since he'd left Washington National Airport.

He decided to try to lose the tail, and as soon as they crossed the bridge, Hogan searched for the first cutoff on his right and spun into it. He raced along Daniel French Drive and twisted the wheel to wrench the car into Independence Avenue and across the Kutz Bridge. Glancing in the mirror, he could see the pursuing vehicle and pushed the pedal to the floor.

Brom gripped the seat fearfully and shouted, "Why are you going so swiftly?"

"Behind you. The danger you sensed is in that brown car."

"Why don't we stop and test their courage?"

"With what? They've probably got the latest in automatic weapons on them."

"We have these." Brom held up the sword, the knife and the assault rifle.

"Any ammo in that gun?"

"I think there are metal pellets left." He reached into a pocket and took out a clip. He held it up for Hogan to see. "And I still have one of these."

Hogan smiled grimly. "For a foreigner, you catch on quick."

He turned the car into Fifteenth Street, and the brown sedan followed.

"Let's find a good place to end this," he said, then twisted the wheel left and sped into Constitution Avenue.

Brom saw a line of people walking toward a low black stone wall. "What is that? A shrine?"

Hogan searched for a good place to come to a stop.

"In a way. It's a memorial to a lot of men and women who died in a war I was in."

"Heroes," the Kalabrian commented.

"Dead heroes. I don't plan to end up like them any sooner than I have to," Black Jack snapped as he pulled the rental car to the curb and jammed on the brakes.

He looked in his rearview mirror. The large sedan was coming up fast. He pointed to the grassy expanse on his left. There was a small stand of trees near the curb.

"We'll open the doors and get behind those trees."

He reached for the AK-47, and Brom was about to hand him the sword.

"We'll switch later," Black Jack growled as they started to fling themselves through the doors.

They had raced for the trees, and from their cover saw the three opponents pile out of the brown vehicle.

The Kalabrian stared at the squat weapons in the hands of the attackers.

"What kind of fire-sticks are those?"

"They put out a lot of those deadly pieces of metal—we call them bullets—very quickly."

"This is your world. How should we handle them?"

Hogan thought quickly. "I don't think they suspect we've got a gun." He thought of something. "Where'd you put the extra clip?"

Brom reached into his pocket. He handed the long metal banana-shaped clip over. Hogan released the clip in the AK-47 and snapped the new one in.

"Why did you do that?"

"Old saying. Better safe than sorry."

Somehow the words made sense to the bearded warrior.

"Do we wait until they get closer?"

"Yes. I'll shoot and you make sure they're dead."

The three hitmen moved cautiously toward the trees, then opened fire simultaneously, chopping deep holes in the hardwood trees. There was no response from behind the trees.

"Let's get closer," the leader shouted, and all three started to rush the trees.

Hogan jumped to his feet and, holding the AK-47 in front of him like a fire hose, squeezed the trigger and sprayed the space in front of him with hot-tempered death-seekers.

Two of the men fell forward with a soft groan, and another one yelped and grabbed his knee. Then one of the wounded men looked up and glared at the target as he raised his automatic to squeeze off a round.

Brom rushed toward him and hacked at his back with all the power in his huge arms. The keen edge of the blade easily cut through the skin and tissues and severed the back of the rib cage and spinal column before the bearded warrior withdrew it.

He stared at the blood-covered blade and wiped it clean on the clothes of the dead man at his feet.

A wounded killer rolled on his side, groaning from the pain of his punctured lungs. He could taste the blood in his mouth, which made it difficult for him to breathe. Hogan squatted next to him and asked in a hard-edged voice, "Who hired you?"

He kept groaning, and Hogan reached over and shook him.

"I asked who hired you."

The dying man spit blood into the warrior's face, then grinned cruelly. A shadow hovered over him. Brom, his face filled with fury, raised his krall high, then threw himself down on the fallen man and skewered him through the neck.

Watching for any signs of life, he withdrew the knife and wiped it clean on the man's shirt, then stood up.

Hogan handed the red-bearded warrior the automatic rifle and the partially filled extra clip, then looked at the blood spurting from the severed throat. "Why did you do that?"

"In Kalabria we kill crazed animals," Brom replied quietly.

The wailing of sirens and the screeching of tires interrupted Black Jack's response. He turned and saw a half-dozen blue-suited policemen running toward them.

"We better get out of here," he snapped, and turned back to Brom.

He was gone. Only the hint of a shimmering cloud remained, but that, too, was already dissipating in the light breeze. But as Hogan sprinted off, he saw swiftly changing images in the puddles that had collected on the sidewalk from a shower earlier in the day. He saw disjointed scenes of mounted men and a great flashing of long, naked swords....

22

The wind had begun to blow its searing breath across Kalabria. Soon it would scream, like the "mindless ones" in battle, as it tried to suck the body fluids from anyone foolish enough to be out in it. Like him, Brom reminded himself.

Mondlock was there to watch as two thousand Kalabrians waited for the fiery-haired warrior to lead them into the high plains where they would face the Sjarik.

"I looked for you last night."

"I was with Hogan."

"And both of you are well."

The bearded warrior nodded, and the two men clasped each other's forearm tightly.

"I shall be back from my retreat on the last day of the Sjarik. Take care of yourself," the Knower said affectionately. "Raikana's men are already out scouring for your warriors."

He put the Kalabrian leader's hand on the pendant he wore under his robe as a mark that he was protected by the gods. It contained a bit of the energy of Ost, the god who created all of the worlds and the family of gods who ruled them.

This was the rarest of honors because usually only the handful of Knowers who were the priests of Ost were permitted to feel his power flow through them.

Mondlock's eyes fell to the long object wrapped in a blanket that Brom had tied to the side of his saddle.

"Hogan's fire-stick. To practice while I wait for the Manhood Tests to end," the bearded leader explained.

Brom's practicing had caused near-riots when he'd fired the long thunder-marker at a large straw form. Hot chunks of metal had narrowly missed soldiers and their rearing mounts when they'd wandered too close to where the red-topped warrior was trying to learn how to control the strange weapon.

One of his slugs almost started a revolution when it drilled into the side of a huge cauldron in which the traditional pre-Sjarik feast was being cooked. Only the quick action of an alert cook, who grabbed a metal spike and hammered it into the hole before much of the stew had been spilled, prevented a violent confrontation between the pro- and anti-firestick Kalabrian warriors.

"Be careful not to hit a cooking pot," the Knower warned with a sly smile, then carefully pulled himself into the saddle and slowly rode away from the camp.

Mora came out of the tent and moved to Brom's side. No words were exchanged between them, only long looks that said more than any words could. She handed him a waterskin filled with a nourishing brew she herself had prepared.

Then he tore his eyes from hers, and his head held high, he led his warriors out of the camp, smiling down at the boys who gaped before the tents.

For half a day the Kalabrian warriors traveled until they reached the northern plains that touched the edges of the Forbidden Region. The wind had increased its velocity. Now it started beating against them. In a short while it would feel like a wall of rock smashing into their bodies and its screams would tear at their sanity as they struggled to survive while they searched for the elusive reptile whose tail they'd pledged to bring home.

The sun had almost ended its shift when they reached the parting place. Here they would separate, each seeking to prove again he was worthy of being called a man.

Brom raised his hands to stop the horses.

He turned and looked at those who had joined him. Like himself, each wore dampened clothes and carried a skin full of nourishing beverage. A rolled blanket was tied to the back of their saddles, and their weapons were strapped to their sides or backs. Some of them, Brom knew, would not return.

"At this time on the morrow, we shall assemble here for the proud return to our homes," the Kalabrian leader shouted. "Bring back the tail of the poison-tongued Galik as proof you were here. Or, if the slimy creatures avoid you, at least bring yourself back."

The men cheered. The Kalabrian leader raised his hand once more for silence.

"And may Sundra bless your Manhood Test."

The men cheered again, then separated to seek their own trophies.

Brom watched as the men rode away, staring after them until they became tiny dots that disappeared into the clouds of dust raised by the wind. He felt a sense of pride in the courage they displayed. It was no secret that Raikana's creatures would probably defy the Sjarik to find and kill as many of the Kalabrian soldiers as they could.

He could feel the temperature rising around him. The Sjarik would explode in full fury before the next day's sun pushed the night out of the sky. Already the screaming wind tore into his eardrums, causing them to quiver in pain.

Wrapping a dampened scarf around his face and head, Brom moved his stallion in the direction of the high hills where he would stop and test his own mortality.

23

Wilson and Hogan stared at each other across the hotel room.

"Just be careful, Jack. Things aren't always what they seem."

"That's for sure," Hogan commented, reflecting on the assault tonight. "Thanks for rescuing me from the Washington police. The question is 'Who knew I was in Washington?'"

"It could have been anybody. Even the White House isn't leakproof."

Wilson had been wondering how anybody had found out Black Jack was coming to Washington or what flight he'd be taking. Only a select handful of people in the White House knew.

He quickly went through the list. The President. His chief of staff. General Paul Robertson and himself.

And, of course, the President's private secretary.

The process of elimination made him conclude that unless it was the President's secretary, Paul Robertson was the leak.

He wondered why, then thought of something else and turned to the man who was sprawled on the king-size bed. "What happened to the gun and knife you used?"

Hogan looked blank. "What gun and knife?"

Wilson shrugged. Black Jack was not going to enlighten him, and there was no point pressing the issue.

As he got up to leave, the white-haired Intelligence officer looked at Hogan.

"That warning I gave you goes for everybody."

"Including you?"

Wilson grinned, then walked out of the room.

IF ANYTHING, Evelyn was more fragile, more beautiful than he remembered her. As he sat across from her at the table in the cozy Georgetown Italian restaurant, Black Jack pretended to listen to her words, but all he could see was her face and his memories.

The Evelyn he had known, the girl who talked incessantly of spirits and ghosts, had become a woman—a beautiful, sensuous-looking woman.

He kept staring at her eyes. There was a message in them that made him hungry and nervous at the same time. "I want you," they seemed to be saying.

As much as his body responded, Jack Hogan wasn't sure he should let her back into his life. Especially now when it might not last a whole lot longer.

The pale blond woman stopped talking and smiled at him. "I don't think you've heard a word I said, Jack."

Even though it was true, he denied it. "You were talking about why you decided to join the United Nations."

Evelyn laughed. "That was ten minutes ago."

Hogan grinned. "You caught me."

She reached out a hand and touched him. "You still have that devilish grin."

Hogan shook his head. "Some things never change." He paused, then went on. "Like you."

"We all change. Even me." She studied his face. "You've changed," she said, then took a breath and added, "for the better. Your face has more, ah, character."

Despite his fascination with her, something was bothering him. Was it because he kept comparing her to the strawberry-haired girl in his mind?

He brought up a more sensitive memory. "Are you still as interested in those mystical cults as you used to be?"

She didn't seem to mind. "They went with the flower girl clothes when I returned to medical school."

He glanced at the pendant around her neck, hanging on a thin gold chain. The peace symbol of the sixties. He had given her one that looked just like that pendant.

"Some things don't go."

She touched the gold circle she wore. "A memory of a long time ago," she answered shyly.

On the flight over, Black Jack had read an article by a police expert in Ohio about the symbols of the new occult cults. "Better be careful. I read that some of the Satan cults are using it as one of their symbols."

Her eyes opened in surprise. "Really. I guess I better pack it away with my other mementos now that I live the quiet life of a doctor."

"Who still insists on sticking her neck out," he reminded her.

She became quiet. "You didn't see the bodies, Jack. I did."

Because they were scheduled to leave on a military jet very early in the morning, Hogan signaled for the check. "We'd better get some sleep. We have to get an early start tomorrow, and there's a long flight ahead of us."

After he'd settled their bill, he escorted her to the door of her suite. For a long time the two of them kept looking at each other. Suddenly Hogan could almost smell the passion of their last day together a long time ago.

He squeezed her hand and turned to leave, then heard her ask in a low intimate tone, "Would you like to come in for a minute?"

24

In the dark of night, the peddler had slipped past the border guards who kept their automatic weapons pointed at the Turkish lands beyond. After finding a cave in which to sleep, he got up, put on his dusty fez, brewed himself a cup of thick Turkish coffee, chewed on some hard bread and started on his tiring journey again.

Leading his three donkeys laden with pots and pans and a hundred other useful utensils along the narrow mountain road, Feyd bemoaned how little he had sold to the Kurdish villagers so far.

A hungry family of five small children and one overweight wife were waiting for him to return with enough money to support them until his next sales trip. All they wanted from him was the money he earned so they could fill their ungrateful bellies, he grumbled to himself.

It was enough to make a man reluctant to ever go home. But he was an honorable man, and it was Ayellah's father who had provided the funds to purchase his inventory. So he would return, but not until he had sold most of the fine utensils he had brought with him and tasted the long-unused pleasures of many more village widows.

His face blanched as he looked around and saw the twin cone towers sticking up in the distance. He had accidentally wandered into the land of the devil worshipers—the Yazidi. His first impulse was to move quickly away from this cursed place. Then practical considerations entered his mind.

Even lovers of Shaitan needed pots and pans for cooking. Of course, he would have to charge them more than he'd gotten from other villagers. After all, he was risking his eternal soul to do business with them, he reminded himself as he started to lead the animals around a large boulder.

Then he heard voices shouting and stopped.

Tying his donkeys to a bush, he peered carefully from behind the huge rock.

Three uniformed soldiers were standing around a shiny new car parked in the middle of the narrow dirt road. Their own car, a dusty military vehicle, had been driven off the road and was parked under a large tree.

A stout man in a sergeant's uniform was yelling at the other two soldiers. "How could you shoot the aide to Colonel Saddam?"

"You ordered me to," the other, a thin small man, protested.

"I told you to stop him, not kill him. The colonel said he wanted him returned alive."

The pockmarked third soldier stared at the body and moaned. "What are we going to do?"

"We don't need your tears, Gamal," the officer said brusquely, then buried his chin in his hand and gave the problem thought. "We could return the body and say the captain tried to escape."

"And end up as guinea pigs for the chemical plant like the accursed Yazidis," came the dire prediction.

The thin man's eyes brightened. "I have an idea. Let's have the captain disappear. That way, the colonel will think he fled across the borders."

"Yes," the sergeant agreed. "But where are we going to hide him?"

The thin man looked around and saw the twin cones peeking from behind the nearby hill. He pointed to it.

"The perfect place. We will hide the body and vehicle inside. Nobody will think of looking for him in there."

The scarred soldier whined again. "And what happens when the Yazidis find him?"

"They won't say a word," the other soldier replied, "because they know they will be blamed for his death."

As Feyd watched, one of the soldiers pushed the body of the dead man over and got in his vehicle. The other two got in the military car. Then all three drove along the road in the direction of the Yazidi shrine.

There was something on the ground where the shiny vehicle had been stopped.

Feyd hastily muttered a prayer and ran up to take a closer look.

It was a large, expensive leather case. Looking around to make sure no one was watching, he grabbed it and ran back to his animals.

Sitting in the shade, he opened it and stared with wonder at the huge number of American hundred-dollar bills inside. Hastily he counted them. There was more than enough to support his whole family for many years.

He dug his hand past the money and found two vials of what looked to be medicine. And a wallet. He checked but it was empty. There were some official-looking documents with pictures.

As he fingered the two vials of medicine, he studied the labels. He didn't know what kind of medicine this was, but he was certain it would cure something.

There were a number of handwritten sheets of paper. Feyd couldn't read, but his cousin in Mardin could. Perhaps they were worth money to somebody.

He shoved the money and the other items into one of the sacks on his lead donkey, then tossed the leather bag behind the bush.

Praising God for his sudden good fortune in—of all places—the home of the Shaitan worshipers who somehow had caused the death of the unfortunate man, the peddler grabbed the reins of the lead animal and headed for the border.

BROM WAS CERTAIN he had actually seen the wind siphon water from the creeks and ground. Small creeks turned to drying mud. Moist, fertile soil became dust that sailed in huge spiral waves at the whim of an insane, howling wind. Tall thick trees stripped of their sap bent and snapped, their loud, explosive protests lost in the louder bansheelike cries of a sky gone mad.

Only the Galik slithered across the plains, dragging its long tail behind it, seeking to immobilize smaller lizards and rodents with venom from its multiple needles.

A huge Tambruk—the fearless four-legged creature that Kalabrian hunters prized for its meat—had gone mad. As Brom watched, the mighty beast rammed its antlers again and again against a large outcropping of rocks, trying to kill the noises in its head. Finally the animal—bloodied from its continual assault on the stones—fell to the ground and let the Sjarik destroy it.

A trio of Galiks crawled out from behind the rocks and cautiously began to chew at the brain tissue that was oozing from the fractured skull of the now-dead creature.

Disgusted at the spectacle, the bearded warrior prodded his horse and got closer, then dismounted. Waiting until the reptiles were too busy feasting to pay attention to anything else, Brom pulled out his krall and moved slowly toward their feeding site.

With one slashing blow, he severed the tail of the nearest Galik and grabbed it with his free hand, then rammed the sharp tip of his knife into the center of the reptile's head, where its tiny brain was hidden.

Quickly Brom dropped the fatty tail in his saddlebag and mounted his animal. Now he had his trophy. If he could survive through the night, he could lead his men back from their face-off with hell.

He prodded his reluctant animal and steered him up the hill. On the other side was the hollow where he would wait out Sundra's wind.

25

For almost an hour, Jack Hogan and the American doctor sat on the couch in her hotel suite and talked about nothing in particular. Then, without warning, Evelyn dropped a soft kiss on his lips. Soon her kiss turned warmer, and despite his reluctance, Hogan felt his resistance fading. He hauled her closer and molded the sinuous body against his in a tight embrace.

Suddenly there was no willingness to wait, and the bed was too far away. They couldn't take their clothes off fast enough, and they merged with a fury built from memories of past encounters.

An impatient hunger sent them tumbling from the couch to the carpeted floor, without interrupting the fulfillment of urgent needs. She wasn't Evelyn. She was a woman on fire and he was being consumed by it.

Finally the two lay on the floor, gasping for air, unable to move.

Evelyn was the first to get to her feet.

"I need a quick shower before we go on," she said, smiling down winsomely. "Do you want to go on?"

Hogan didn't answer. He wasn't sure.

"I'll be right out," she said as she closed the door to the bathroom.

There was the sound of running water, and Hogan picked up his clothes and planted himself on the couch. He was physically satisfied, but not happy. He had a strange, uncomfortable feeling being here with Evelyn.

Maybe he'd been shaken by discovering her again. He glanced at the large bowl of fresh fruit the hotel management had sent up as a welcome gift. He needed something to moisten the dryness in his mouth. He was already reaching for an orange when he stopped himself. He knew he was avoiding the truth. His dry mouth didn't bother him. Being with Evelyn did.

He was tempted to put on his clothes and leave. Then he remembered they would be traveling together. No he decided, he'd better stay.

He let his eyes close. She would expect a rematch when she came out. Given what he'd gone through in the preliminary round, he needed to revive his energies.

HOGAN HAD ALMOST dozed off when the hair of his nape started to prickle. Someone else was there with him. He started groping for a weapon, then remembered he had carried none.

Even his pocket was gone, he realized. He was naked. Bracing himself to leap at the intruder, he opened his eyes.

He saw a kind of glowing that outlined a red beard in the dark.

It was Brom.

In his hands the warrior held the howling sword as he looked around the room. A scarf was wrapped loosely around his mouth, and his eyes looking menacing above it.

Black Jack whispered, "What the hell are you doing here?"

The Kalabrian stared at the American's naked body, then lowered the scarf. "I sensed you were in danger, Hogan."

Hogan grabbed his clothes and started putting them on. "Does it look like I'm in danger?"

Brom shook his head. "No, it doesn't seem so." He looked around. "Where is the woman?"

Hogan pointed to the closed bathroom door. "In there, washing herself between rounds."

The warrior groaned. "Do all of you people have this strange need to wash themselves all the time?"

"Never mind. Can you get out of here before she comes out?"

"I would like to see one of the women of your world closer."

"Some other time," Hogan hissed.

Brom stalked around the room, examining the furniture as Hogan pulled on his clothes. He turned back to the American. "What kind of place is this we are in?"

"It's called a hotel suite," Hogan said, realizing then the Kalabrian would have nothing he could compare. "Like many houses put together for people who journey from their homes."

The redheaded man made a face. "Too small. And very stuffy. Don't your people like the air that Sundra gave them?"

Despite his irritation at Brom's sudden appearance, Hogan smiled. "Not much. We prefer what we call air conditioning."

He walked over to the window unit and turned it on. Frigid air began to fill the room.

Quivering with delight, the Kalabrian leader stood in front of it and let the chilled air wash across him.

"This is more magic, like your fire-sticks. If only I could take one back with me."

Hogan was about to answer when he heard the bathroom door handle turning.

He pointed to the wall alongside the door. "Quick," he whispered, "against that wall. When she comes out, I'll keep her busy while you do your vanishing act."

The door swung open. Evelyn stood there, dewy looking and glowing. Her robe hung open, revealing the soft roundness of her breasts, the small patch of dark blond hair at the apex of her thighs.

And the automatic in her hand.

Hogan was stunned.

"It's been nice, but you are interfering with a greater destiny," she intoned flatly as she pointed the weapon at his chest, but she didn't have time to pull the trigger.

The howling sword sang a song of death as it slashed through the air and severed her entire arm from her body. As if she couldn't believe what had just happened, the pale blond woman shouted the word that was meant to accompany the fatal shot. "Die!"

Then she fell into the puddle of blood that had run from her ruptured veins and arteries, and softly cried out for help.

"Satan come and take me to your bosom."

Over and over she repeated the phrase, until her voice faded and stopped.

Hogan turned away from the inert body and stared at Brom. He was just stunned. Not long ago she had been in his arms, then she'd shown herself ready to kill the same body she'd held so close to her own—and now she was no more. "How did you know?"

Brom shrugged. "I didn't." He glanced at the now-still body. "You choose strange women companions."

"Yeah." He still didn't understand why she wanted to kill him. "I better call Wilson."

"This king of yours?"

"My boss," Hogan said as he went to the phone and quickly dialed a number.

Wilson answered at last, sounding half-asleep. Black Jack told him what had happened, omitting mention of the Kalabrian.

"I'm taking a powder for twenty-four hours until you get this handled," Hogan said, then hung up before the Intelligence officer could ask questions. He'd let the Intel wizard try to figure out how a sword got into Evelyn's suite.

"I'm going with you," he said to the Kalabrian as he gingerly squatted down and grabbed the automatic from the unattached arm.

Brom tore the sheets from the bed and disappeared into the bathroom, only to call for Hogan's help with the water faucets. When he got the sheets wet, he handed one to Hogan. "Wrap this around you," he ordered.

They were standing close together when a faint glimmering swirled in the air around them....

THE KALABRIAN WIND tore at Hogan's body with unrelenting fury.

"The Sjarik," Brom shouted.

"I know," Black Jack yelled back. "You mean men go out in this deliberately?"

"It is how we prove we are warriors."

"There's got to be an easier way."

Black Jack wondered why he had chosen to return with the red-bearded warrior. He could have found a less miserable place to take cover until Wilson used his influence to explain the incident in Evelyn Thomas's suite.

"There is no better way for brave men," Brom shouted.

The sand whipped against their faces, rushing through every narrow opening to cut into their skins.

Hogan tapped the Kalabrian on the arm. When Brom turned and faced him, Hogan shouted a question. "What do we do now that we're here?"

"Wait."

"For what?"

"For the Manhood Tests to be finished."

Hogan knew that if Astrah was right, that meant he had to be out in this demented storm until morning.

The Kalabrian handed him a water-skin. "Drink. It is nourishing. Mora prepared it."

Black Jack took a sip. The broth tasted strange, but it seemed to course through his veins and renew him. He looked at the other man. "Do we have to stand?"

"No. Why?"

"Then I'm going to sit down."

Hogan eased his body to the ground and leaned his back against a huge boulder. He felt bone tired, but not so much by the vigorous mating as by the shocked emotions that had left him drained.

The bearded Kalabrian slid down beside him.

"This is how true warriors test themselves," Brom shouted, grinning. "Do you not find it exciting?"

Hogan stared at the bending trees and flying dust and groaned. Just his luck. He had a spiritual twin who badly needed psychiatric help.

THE VELOCITY OF THE WIND was increasing. So was the temperature. Brom's horse, tethered to the lowest limb of a quivering hardwood tree, shivered with fear.

Sitting with their backs to the boulders, Brom and Hogan were waiting out the screaming storm by trying to nap.

A huge burst of rushing air pounded at the hardwood tree, ramming it from every side until the thick wood surrendered and splintered at the base. The reins fell free and the horse neighed loudly as the tree toppled and crashed.

Brom opened his eyes and saw his mount rear up and start to race away in panic. He elbowed Hogan and jumped to his feet.

"It's a long walk back to camp. We have to catch him."

The two warriors threw themselves into the storm and chased after the terrified animal as it charged to the crest of the hill.

Fighting the walls of wind before them, the two pressed to reach the animal.

All around the frightened mount, trees were felled by the fury of the wind. The huge animal turned and started galloping back at Brom and Hogan.

Terror dominated the horse's actions. Brom jumped out of its way as it galloped past him, then the creature swung and headed for Hogan.

Bracing himself, the American waited until the spooked creature was almost past him, then jumped and grabbed the front of the saddle.

Hanging on determinedly, Black Jack let the animal drag him thirty yards, then threw his body onto the top of the horse and twisted himself into the saddle.

Meanwhile Brom jumped in front of the still-panicked animal and waved his arms in front of it. Rearing its legs high in the air, the huge mount whinnied angrily as the rider on his back reached down and grabbed the reins.

The gentle pulling of the bit in his mouth seemed to calm the animal enough for the Kalabrian to pat it.

"You ride well, Hogan," he shouted.

Black Jack was about to repay the compliment when he looked down the hill and saw the large party of enemy soldiers. He gestured to Brom and dismounted.

Together they crawled to the crest and peered down. More than thirty foot-soldiers and three armored men on horseback were gathered in a crude circle. But they weren't the ones who captured Hogan's attention—it was the white-haired boy being led away at sword point.

THE STERN-FACED MAN LED the white-haired boy around the large boulders until they were alone. Then he leaned down from his horse, and his expression changed as he shouted, "Run, boy, until you find some of your own kind."

For a moment the boy looked puzzled. Then confusion turned to gratitude and he began to race away.

Over the shrieking wind, the soldier heard somebody behind shout. "Traitor!"

He turned and saw the rage-filled face of his captain, Vaka, as the bull of a man galloped his mount at him. He leaned forward in his saddle and whipped the reins against his animal's body to urge it to greater speed and take him far away—if he could make it.

Then he felt a burning agony as the tip of a long sword punctured a hole in his back and sliced his lung in two.

His large body fell from the saddle and panicked the horse, who galloped away, dragging the still form that held the reins in a death lock.

The boy turned as he ran and saw the towering mounted figure charge at him with raised blade. Quickly looking around, he could see no place where he could safely hide. From under his shirt, he pulled out a large knife and raised it as he had seen the Kalabrian soldiers do in practice drills.

The captain sneered as he reached the white-haired child and slashed his sword down at him. The boy waited for his chance, then, gripping the knife with both hands as Lord Brom had done with the howling sword, whipped it at the wrist that held the bloodied long blade.

Screaming with outrage and pain, Vaka pulled his mount to a sudden halt and leaped from his saddle to run toward the boy.

HE WAS TOO FAR AWAY to save the boy, but Black Jack started running. At least he could kill the bastard who had raised his sword to a child.

"W-a-i-t!" Brom shouted while he tore the blanket-wrapped packet from the rear of his saddle.

The American paused briefly and looked back, and Brom raced forward and threw the object at Hogan. "Here!" he yelled.

Through the blanket, Hogan could feel the familiar shape of the AK-47. He tore the covers off and glanced at it.

The clip was still in it.

He turned and raced down the hill. Below he could see the boy dart out of the way as the officer attempted to run him through with his steel. Jerking a round into the chamber, Black Jack aimed behind the soldier and let go an angry burst.

VAKA WAS STUNNED at the loud explosion behind him. His first thought was that the accursed Sjarik had shattered several more trees.

Then he looked up at the hill and saw the strange warrior charging through the clouds of whirling dust at him.

He recognized the weapon in his hands. A fire-stick. This was no warrior. This was the violent Kalabrian god who vented his revenge on Raikana's soldiers.

Terrified, Vaka ran back to his mount and started to climb into the saddle when he saw the huge bearded warrior appear at his side.

It was Brom, the man Vaka had been searching for through most of the day. Now he was here, with his sword drawn.

Fighting the gale, the armored captain shoved his sword in front of him and parried the Kalabrian's slashing blow. Steel clanging against steel, the clashing swords rang loudly over the bellowing wind as the duelers parried and thrust, then switched to slashing and jabbing.

Suddenly, as if he were teaching a lesson in swordsmanship, Brom paused momentarily and raised the howling sword before his face, acting as if the blustering skies were not present.

Vaka watched, bewildered, wondering why the Kalabrian leader was posing.

The red-beard grinned cruelly, then whipped his body in a full circle as the armored captain watched in hypnotized amazement, and threw all of his weight behind his next drive.

The howling sword skewered the bull of a man as it slid cleanly through the base of his stomach. Vaka's eyes widened in terror as Brom jerked the blade up, then fell to his knees, holding his abdomen to keep his innards from spilling onto the dust-covered ground.

THE TWO SERGEANTS who had traveled with Captain Vaka charged around the boulders and came face-to-face with the strange warrior who held an oddly shaped weapon in front of him.

One of them recognized him. "Komar," he screamed, trying to turn his horse around.

Hogan braced his widespread legs and washed the space in front of him with a long burst of death-seekers. Torn to rags by the hot lead, the soldiers' bodies slid from the saddle to the ground as their frightened horses turned and ran into a cloud of dust.

There was no time for Hogan to think about anything except that more than thirty painted savages had started to charge him.

"Let's get out of here," he shouted over the wind.

"Too late," he heard Brom yell back.

Hogan fired a short burst at the oncoming horde, then watched as panic and puzzlement twisted their faces. They looked bewildered, as though they had been awakened from a dream only to find themselves face-to-face with their worst nightmares.

Screaming in terror, the painted Jaddueii turned and took off in a panicked headlong flight.

Brom moved to Hogan's side and tried to blink the wind-driven sand from his eyes as the two watched the foot soldiers vanish into the swirling sand.

His storm-beaten face was filled with an expression of surprise. "I've never seen the mindless ones run away without a signal," he said.

"Whatever their queen does to keep them under control doesn't last long," Black Jack agreed, yelling to make himself heard over the wailing gusts.

Then both of them thought of the boy and turned to see the white-haired child move timidly to their side. Hogan smiled at him reassuringly.

Brom looked down at the child. "Who are you, little man, and how did you get here?"

"I'm Timur from the village...the last of my line...so I wanted to come and join the men. I have no father and I wanted to grow up faster." Suddenly he grinned. "We showed them how Kalabrian warriors can fight, didn't we?"

Hogan and Brom exchanged glances, then Brom leaned closer to the small boy.

"Yes, we showed them," he said loudly. Sweeping the child up into his huge arms, he added, "Let's go find you a Galik so you can bring his tail home and proclaim you a warrior."

He turned to wink at his twin, but Black Jack was gone.

26

Hogan stared out of the window of the military cargo plane he'd boarded in Ankara. Spread out below was the fascinating mixture of Arabic and Western architecture. The small Turkish city of Mardin looked deceptively calm and peaceful. Even from that height, he thought he could almost hear the singsong voices of the mullahs calling the faithful to prayer.

The jeep and the two huge canvas bags filled with supplies were flying with him. So was the gift from Brom, safely packed in one of the bags. Wilson had come through, though all through the previous day in Washington he'd had to dodge the man's endless questions. Finally Wilson gave up knowing any more details of Evelyn's death and hustled Hogan onto a military jet to Turkey. There was still Operation Fuse Point to think of.

Ten minutes until landing. Ten minutes to continue pondering questions to which he had no answers.

Why had Evelyn tried to kill him? Wilson had been mystified by the manner of her death, but had arranged to have her body whisked from her hotel suite in the middle of the night. But he had no explanation for motive, either.

The one thing that had become glaringly clear was that something bigger than the white-haired Intelligence officer had originally outlined was going on, and Hogan was right in the middle of it.

Perhaps the free-lance agent he was due to meet on landing would have a clue. Hogan had flown to Ankara because the agent had contacted the CIA chief of station in Ankara, alluding to important information about something that was going on across the border for sale.

"THE NAME IS Enver Riza," the stout man said, enthusiastically pumping Hogan's hand. He grabbed Black Jack's small suitcase and shoved it in the trunk of the ancient Volkswagen, then opened the passenger door. "Come get in. We can talk while we drive."

He kept talking as he raced the surprisingly fast car around corners. His cousin, the fez-topped man explained, was a traveling seller of utensils who had returned from an illegal sales journey across the border a few days ago.

"Sometimes," he explained, his eyes twinkling in his bearded face as he turned his head to Hogan, "a man has to break a few rules to support his family. The border guards of our neighbor are not friendly."

The driver of an oncoming Mercedes truck spun his wheel to avoid a head-on collision.

"Uh, you could keep your eye on the road while you're talking," the American visitor suggested.

"Of course, of course," the driver quickly agreed, wiping perspiration from his forehead with the sleeve of his sweat-stained shirt. Taking a deep breath, he continued his explanation. "My cousin happened to be on a sales trip and saw some soldiers hiding the body of a man. Being curious, he waited until they left and checked around."

"Who was the dead man?"

Enver Kiza handed him a wallet. Black Jack checked through the pockets. Money and credit cards were gone. All that remained were some engraved calling cards and a military ID.

A face stared up at him, and it didn't take long to recognize the man. And his name was there, clearly typed.

Hogan remembered the name from Wilson's files. Khalid was Saddam's personal aide, and Black Jack wondered why he had been killed.

He turned to the driver. "Were there any papers?"

"Yes." He handed several folded sheets to the American. "These."

Black Jack scanned the words and whistled. Although the language was somewhat veiled, it revealed everything Wilson had suspected, and more. Saddam was planning a series of wars with his neighbors that could involve the rest of the world. The chemical he was manufacturing, TX-133, was going to be his way of reducing resistance to his invasion.

Hogan's face became stony as he read about the international bankers who were backing Saddam. Such men didn't deserve to live.

The Turkish driver glanced at him and saw the fury in his face.

"Is something wrong?"

Black Jack didn't answer. He kept staring at the mention of confidential information being given to Saddam by some general in Washington. If he could find out who it was, there wouldn't be enough of him left to bury.

He had to get the information to Washington, but the problem was that the document really contained only one man's word—and that man was dead.

The driver looked at him hopefully. "It is worth something to your government?"

"If we can prove the information correct. What else did your cousin find?"

Enver Riza waved the question away with a languid gesture. "Some odds and ends. Nothing important."

"What were they?"

The free-lance agent glanced at the expression on the face of the man next to him. Its coldness made him shiver despite the heat of the day.

"Some money and two small vials of medicine. That's all."

"The vials—where are they?"

The driver looked relieved that the American hadn't asked how much money had been found. "At my cousin's home."

"Take me there."

Riza didn't argue. He aimed his tired vehicle toward Feyd's small house.

GULEK GLANCED at his older brothers and sisters, who were playing with the two vials their father had brought with him, pretending they were great scientists.

Ahmed, the oldest, was baby-sitting while their parents were out shopping. Imitating one of the teachers in his school, he made a fuss over his ability to read the labels on the vials. "This is TX-133." He held it high above his head. "I have discovered this great medicine which will cure all illnesses."

The other children laughed and cheered.

He emptied one of the vials into a clean jar. Adding an inch of water from the sink, he looked at his siblings.

"Who will be the first to test my great discovery?"

The others shook their heads and stuck their tongues out at him. He stared a them with disdain.

"Someday, when I am rich and famous, you will be sorry you weren't willing to test my first discovery."

"You test it yourself if you're so smart," Gulek shouted.

The others joined in. "Yes, test it yourself."

Ahmed hesitated. Their father hadn't told him what was in the vial. But as he glanced at the label, he decided it had been made by a manufacturer of medicines, so it certainly couldn't do any harm.

Quickly he lifted the jar to his mouth and swallowed the mixture. After all, he was the oldest and had to set a good example for the others.

His brothers and sisters waited to see if anything happened to him. So did Ahmed.

After ten minutes he still felt fine, and they started playing a new game. Ahmed turned away from the game and pressed his hands against his ears as if he were trying to drown out some painful noise. Then he ran to the kitchen counter, grabbed a large butcher's knife and turned back to the others.

THE STONY-FACED Turkish police captain ordered Hogan and the free-lance agent out of the building while he conducted an investigation.

"You will wait outside until I am ready to question you," he told Black Jack, pointing a thick index finger in his face.

Hogan couldn't stop thinking of the massacre he had discovered in the apartment. Though he'd been stunned, he'd noticed and managed to pocket the vials before he wandered out of what had become a terrible place of mourning.

While Enver Riza and he waited on the street, Black Jack thought about the countless people who had reacted the same as the stunned child.

Later, after the police had let him go with the warning not to leave the city without permission, he called Ankara.

The American Embassy official had promised to get the dead man's notes and the other items to Wilson in Washington by courier.

It was time for Wilson to move in, or to give further direction to Hogan. Clearly there was a madman at work who would stop at nothing to gain his ends—ends which would inevitably affect America and perhaps even draw it into war.

27

Colonel Saddam was livid. "How could the American doctor disappear?"

The blond man sitting across the desk from him had been wondering about that ever since he had tried to call Dr. Evelyn Thomas at the hotel in Washington, only to be told she had checked out the day before.

"It doesn't make sense," the irate Arab ruler shouted as he got to his feet. "One of my best men from the embassy followed them."

He checked the notes in his hand.

"First they went to dinner. Then they returned to her hotel. Neither Hogan nor the doctor ever came out."

"How long did your man watch the hotel?"

"Until almost dawn."

Nis wondered if she had skipped taking the drug he had given her. That was the only logical explanation for her failure to follow his instructions.

He looked up at the still-enraged man.

"Perhaps they left together by a rear door."

"No, he checked. The police had cordoned off the rear of the building to allow an ambulance to take a guest of the hotel to a local hospital. The only way out of the hotel was the front door."

Nis pursed his lips. Now he understood why he no longer sensed her life aura. She was the guest the ambulance had been sent to get. The American doctor was dead.

Calmly he asked, "What about the American agent?"

"Vanished."

The Oriental-featured blond man nodded. Or gone to another world, he acknowledged the likelihood silently. He would have Raikana order her men to search for him.

The impeccably dressed colonel slammed his fist down on the desk and interrupted Nis's thoughts.

"We are only a week away from the realization of a great dream, and everything is going wrong! Khalid is still missing and . . ."

Nis stopped him. "Any indication where he's gone?"

"Like this Hogan, he has vanished."

"Deserted?"

"Nuri Khalid is loyal to me," Saddam replied, offended at the implication he would have a traitor as his aide.

"Are you sure?"

"Of course I am. I had him watched day and night."

"Have you talked to whoever was keeping an eye on him?"

"I questioned him personally. He saw Nuri come out of his apartment, wearing casual clothes, get in his car and drive away. Khalid never wore his uniform when he was visiting one of his foreign mistresses. He wanted them to love him for himself, not for his power."

"How do you know your spy is telling the truth?"

"Our men have their methods," he said with a dismissive shrug.

The blond man paused before asking his next question. "I come back to my earlier question about Khalid. Do you think he has deserted?"

A set look descended on the colonel's face. "No. If he had, the Americans would know of my plans. And Hogan would be here trying to stop them."

WILSON WANDERED into Robertson's office and closed the door behind him. "Got a minute?"

The retired general looked up and smiled. "For you? Anytime."

"There's a problem."

Robertson leaned forward across his desk. "How can I help?"

"Seems there's a leak in the White House. Somebody's been feeding information to Colonel Omar Saddam about our plans for him."

The general could feel the color drain from his face. "Do you have any idea who it is?"

"A damned good one. Seems Saddam's aide, Nuri Khalid, had some notes outlining Saddam's plans and naming who was helping him."

"There were reasons...I can explain," Robertson started to stutter, but Wilson got up and opened the door.

"I'm not the one you have to explain to," he said.

The lanky man behind the desk wore a frantic expression on his face. He could already taste the bitterness of a public trial.

"Is there anything I can do to, ah, make up for it?"

Wilson shrugged. "I'd hate for the White House to be involved in a scandal." He thought for a moment. "How's your health, Paul? Somebody said your doctor had told you it wasn't too good."

Wilson left, closing the door behind him, and Robertson stared fixedly at the portrait of George Washington that hung on the wall.

What was it that the first President was supposed to have said as a child? He remembered: "I cannot tell a lie. I chopped down the cherry-tree."

He glanced at the photograph of his dead wife, grateful she was not alive at this moment. And grateful that they never did have children.

Wilson had said something about ill health. What was he trying to say?

Suddenly Robertson understood. He took one of the pens from the set his aides had given him when he'd retired and wrote a brief note.

Then he opened a side drawer and took out his old Colt Commander .45 ACP automatic. He gently jacked a round into the chamber. Leaning back in his chair, he opened his mouth and pushed the muzzle inside.

AFTER LEAVING the retired general, Hiram Wilson had hurried to the confidential meeting with the senior Intelligence officers of three Middle Eastern embassies. Only the President and he knew about it.

He reviewed Captain Nuri Khalid's notes and shook his head. "We have no proof that what he wrote is true."

"It fits with everything we have learned about Saddam," remarked one of the men at the table, a bearded man who posed as a retired professor in his country.

"What concerns me is the drug TX-133," another said in a worried voice.

"Our scientists are analyzing it now. What they've come up with so far is that it works on the neuro system and makes the user acutely receptive to suggestions. The drug's influence lasts as long as forty-eight hours, and during that period, those under the drug's influence will carry out suggestions that have been planted in their minds."

"Surely that does not explain the behavior of the child in Turkey," said the third man at the table, a former United Nations ambassador for his country.

"The doctors who have been testing the drug think that when someone who has not been prepared with suggestions takes the drug, there is one of two reactions. Complete passivity, or extreme violence."

"Is there an antidote?"

"We're working on one."

"What still bothers me," one of the Intelligence officers at the table said, "is how Saddam plans to get our people to take this drug."

The American shook his head. "We don't know."

"In which case," the retired professor said, standing up, "I should alert my government to keep a close watch on our borders."

"All of you better do that," Wilson suggested quietly.

LATER, WILSON WAS SITTING alone in his office, speculating on just who Dr. Alexander Nis really was, when the phone rang.

He decided to take the call himself. "Wilson."

The caller was a former associate at the Central Intelligence Agency—Hedley Tyson, one of the deputy directors.

"I ran a check on those bankers. All of them have left on extended business trips abroad."

So the rich rats had gone into hiding until after Saddam makes his move, Wilson thought.

While he listened to the details of the report, the white-haired man added their names to a "must-see" list.

Hogan had many people to round up—people who had a lot to answer for.

28

For the past two hours Black Jack had been driving the jeep along the narrow mountain road that looked down on the turquoise blue waters of the Tigris River. Besides the .45 ACP Colt Commander holstered at his waist, he was equipped with the gift knife from Brom, honed to shaving sharpness, and four 40 mm fragmentation and incendiary grenades. In his pockets were a half-dozen clips of ammunition.

On the floor next to him was a CAR-15 assault rifle with a 30-round clip, one round jacked into the chamber and ready to cough its message of death.

He had taken the circuitous route to avoid running into Saddam's border guards, who would insist on inspecting the bags he carried in the back seat.

He wondered how they'd react to the contents: another CAR-15, a dozen 30-round clips for the assault rifles and the Colt, more grenades, timers, plastic explosives and an assortment of tools and supplies.

Several times he had seen pockets of uniformed men in the brightly colored turbans of Saddam's military. They certainly looked well armed and well prepared.

The Arab ruler had turned it into a concentration camp. From everything Wilson had told him, resistance to his insane hunger for power had been virtually eliminated by murder and blackmail. Even the Kurds, noted for their independence and violent opposition to domination, had been slaughtered by the colonel's troops.

Saddam's sudden rise to power was the result of a coup he had engineered against the emir, whose family had ruled the tiny country for almost a thousand years. In a brutal attack the military officer had murdered the emir, his wife and children and all the rest of the ruler's family. Then he blamed their deaths on so-called infidels and declared a holy war against them, with himself at the head of it.

Saddam had promised his people he would turn the country into a paradise. As Black Jack looked around at the parched land surrounding him, he wondered how the colonel defined the word.

He checked his wristwatch. He had four hours to go before he'd reach the capital city, Qatir, where the chemical plant was located, as well as Saddam's palace.

He would have to find a place where he could safely park his vehicle and put together a quick meal. This would be his last chance to eat in the next twenty-four hours.

The road spiraled up along the edge of a rock-cluttered mountain. Maintaining a fifty-mile-per-hour average, Hogan moved the wheel expertly, anticipating each turn without a screech of the tires.

A half-hidden cutoff ahead caught his eye. He pulled the jeep into it and stopped. Perhaps he could find a clear stream nearby for fresh water. It would taste better than the water in his large canteen, which had become tepid.

Getting out of the jeep, Hogan grabbed his CAR-15 and stomped his feet until the knots in his legs were gone, then cautiously strolled along the dirt road.

Over the top of the next hill, he could see the twin cones of a temple. There was something vaguely familiar about it.

Then he remembered Evelyn Thomas's description.

This was where the Yazidi slaughter had taken place.

He started to make his way back to the jeep when he heard the bells.

He stopped when he saw the sea of white sheep crossing the road behind him. He turned and watched them straggle past him, searching for grass.

Behind them walked a young girl wearing a robe with a veil covering half of her face. She used a long stick to prod lagging sheep into keeping up with the rest of the flock.

The large dog by her side growled at Hogan, and she stopped to stare at him. He could see the fear in her eyes.

He called out the traditional Arabic greeting with a smile. "Greetings. Peace be with you."

Shyly the girl replied in like fashion and patted the growling dog to calm him.

Hogan knew enough Arabic to conduct a simple conversation.

"Is there a village nearby?"

"Yes." She pointed up the narrow road, then looked at him with mournful eyes. "But everyone in it is dead."

"I'm sorry. I was just looking for a well."

She shook her head. "Go elsewhere. That well is cursed by Shaitan."

The flock of sheep were already disappearing over the hill, and she and the dog turned and ran after them.

Black Jack ignored the warning and continued his journey up the road.

A few miles ahead he came to the deserted village, a cluster of stone and mud huts circling a rock-rimmed well. He glanced down into the deep well.

Even from the top, the water smelled fresh and cold.

He lowered a crude wooden pail on a rope until he heard its splash, then jiggled the cord. When it felt heavier, he carefully pulled up the bucket.

Staring at the clear, clean-looking water, Hogan decided the fear that Satan had contaminated the well was based on superstition, not fact. He lifted the bucket to his mouth and was about to take a drink when he remembered the glass jar the dazed boy in Mardin had used.

Had the devil poisoned the water?

Suddenly it became obvious. Water.

The shepherd girl had said the water had been cursed by Satan. He'd give odds the same had been true in Namibia.

But who was the devil's representative on earth—or one of many incarnations? Was it Saddam?

Built into the jeep was a powerful shortwave transceiver preset to a frequency monitored by Wilson's people. Hogan ran all the way back to the vehicle and turned on the set.

It was more than just a hunch, he informed the voice on the other end. "Wilson will know to pass the word to higher circles, so there will be some preparedness," he said, then added, "And tell him I'm on my way to send Saddam and Dr. Nis to visit their ancestors—and make sure there's a permanent shortage of water additives."

After he shut down the set, Hogan began to shiver. Now he remembered where else he'd heard the name Nis.

From Brom, Lord of Kalabria.

Only Brom had called him Nis the magician.

What was he dealing with this time? He'd already had two run-ins with the devil. Was this his third time at bat?

The time for reflection was past. He heard sound of gunfire.

29

Two grinning soldiers were firing continuous steel-jacket rounds from their Galil assault rifles at the flock of sheep as if they were practicing at an amusement-park shooting gallery.

Soon their three companions joined them, laughing joyously at the site of large balls of gray-white wool stained dark red with the blood.

As the American warrior watched from behind a large rock, the five men walked through the killing field, pointing their weapons down and spraying lead at the shuddering wooly bodies.

Finally they stopped. Only the fading mournful sounds of animals dying filled the air.

The uniformed men looked at each other's bloodstained clothes and broke into laughter again. Speaking in Arabic they teased one another.

"Now we are going to have to change clothes," one of them said, making the others chortle.

Another looked around. "What happened to the child and her dog?"

One of the troopers searched through the white bodies and called, "They are here, lying next to each other."

They all stood around, looking at the slain child. One of them spit at her body.

"She was only a Kurd."

"So was her dog, I bet," another said, smirking at the thought.

"The world is rid of another of the fierce mountain people," one of the other soldiers commented.

"And we," the fifth chimed in, "have gotten in a little more practice before we cross the borders."

Wrapping their arms around one another, they marched off the field and headed to the road where two military vehicles were parked.

HOGAN UNDERSTOOD what they had said. Stone faced, he waited until they were out of sight, then ran up the hill and looked for the child's body.

He looked down and saw her pitifully tiny form, torn open by the lead from the killer soldiers. The cold anger he felt inside clouded Black Jack's face. This was the same little girl to whom he had wished peace only minutes earlier.

Gripping his CAR-15 tightly, he started to head in the direction the five uniformed murderers had taken when he heard the voices of the soldiers coming closer again. He halted his forward motion, and threw himself on the ground, braced his weapon and waited.

One by one they appeared, and from their loud calls Hogan knew they had come back to search for something.

Black Jack forced himself to be patient until he had all of them in sight, then opened fire. A short burst of hellfire slammed two of the soldiers to the ground, and the remaining three scattered behind the rocks.

Hogan jumped to his feet and retreated behind a boulder. He had plans for the rest of them, and they didn't include living a long time.

To his left he saw a flash of uniform next to a pile of rocks. A burst of lead from his weapon halted any further movement.

Poised to respond instantly, the American warrior waited for Saddam's men to make the first move.

Minutes of silence passed, then a body slithered through the tall grass at him.

Hogan rose to his feet and dug a trench of lead with a long burst from his CAR-15. He was certain he had at least wounded the man. Why hadn't he cried out in pain?

He stared at the tall grass again and saw the reason.

Brom was lying beside the body, withdrawing his kra from the dead soldier's back.

The red-bearded warrior stood and waved at Hogan. H was holding the AK-47 and his long knife in his hands. H howling sword was sheathed in the scabbard on his back.

"Get down, you crazy Kalabrian," Black Jack shouted

Brom looked at him with a questioning expression, but long burst from behind the rocks answered him. Withou hesitation the warrior dove to the ground.

Hogan looked across the hill. "Are you okay?"

"Yes. Where are the enemy?"

"One of them is behind the rock. The other has moved u the hill behind me," Black Jack shouted.

"No, he hasn't. Unless a man without a head can move."

Hogan threw up his hands in surrender. The Kalabria had a way of coming up with simple solutions to difficu problems.

Brom called out again. "Which one of us will have th honor of killing the one behind the rock?"

"This isn't a game."

"All right," the bearded man decided. "We'll both tak him."

In just a few minutes a form leaped out from the protec tion of a boulder and took off in a crouching flight.

"I see him," Brom shouted, and started running after th soldier.

Hogan had to really exert himself to try to catch up wit the bearded warrior. Before he did, Brom had come to stop in the middle of the road and fired his AK-47 at th fleeing military vehicle the soldier had managed to reach.

Lead kept bouncing off the metal sides. One ricochete and tore into the back of the driver's head and drilled int his brain tissue. Falling forward, the man released his grip on the steering wheel. The vehicle lurched ahead as the dead man's foot pressed down on the gas pedal, then ran up the hill and turned over.

The car and dead driver came tumbling down the hill and landed on the narrow road.

The two warriors checked to make sure the man was dead. Brom stared at the overturned vehicle.

"This would be very useful in my land," he said, studying the car with admiration. Then he shook his head. "But where would I find the food to feed it?" He turned to Hogan and said with a smile, "Some things are better off left where they belong."

He looked down at the weapon in his hand. "Except this," he added.

Hogan nodded his agreement. "Thanks for the help."

"After you left, Mondlock the Knower warned me if something happens to you, it may also happen to me."

Hogan groaned. "That makes me feel really good."

The Kalabrian looked around. "This looks like our Forbidden Region. What is this place?"

Black Jack glanced around at the bodies. "Hell."

He remembered the child on the hill. "I've got something to do."

Brom followed him up the hill, clearly overcome by disgust as he stared at the dozens of slain sheep, then looked down at the slight body. "No older than the boy we rescued," he said in anger. "What manner of creatures would slay a small girl?"

Hogan's reply was short and ice-cold. "The kind that don't deserve to live."

He handed the bearded man his weapon and knelt down. Lifting the small body, he stood up and started walking up the hill.

Then he stopped and turned back to his bearded twin.

"Bring the dog's body."

THE TWO WARRIORS STOPPED in front of the large doors to the shrine. Hogan stepped forward and placed the body on the steps. He turned and took the dog from the bearded warrior, then placed it next to the little girl.

Brom lowered his voice. "What building is this?"

"A shrine. I don't know if it's dedicated to the god the little girl believed in, but it will have to do."

"And the dog?"

"He protected her when she lived. Perhaps he'll do the same for her now."

Hogan started to stalk off, then stopped to turn back and look at the Kalabrian. "I've got one more thing to do. Care to join me?"

Brom shook his head. "Your summons came just as I was getting my warriors ready to march against the mad woman in Tella." His voice softened. "We could use your help, Hogan."

"I'll be there if I can," the American promised.

"And I for you."

The two men grasped each other's arm, a gesture that showed their respect for each other and recognized the bond between them. Then Brom moved back and let the shimmering cloud that suddenly appeared surround him.

30

He had taken personal charge of the army, Saddam explained to the six foreign guests who sat in the gaily decorated reviewing stand with him, to make sure the invasions were swift and successful.

"Twenty-five thousand of the finest trained soldiers the Middle East has ever seen," he boasted.

Below them a sea of men paraded by the tall stand, built at the side of the presidential palace. Battalion after battalion stepped smartly in precise cadence, dressed in camouflage fatigues. Each of them gripped an almost nine-pound gas-operated Galil 5.56 mm assault rifle in his hands.

"The finest automatic weapon the Israelis have ever made," the colonel bragged. "And one of the most expensive."

The Swiss banker looked surprised. "You buy from the Israelis?"

"Not directly," Saddam explained quickly.

"Still, I thought you despised them."

"I do. They will be run into the sea to drown like rats," he shouted. Calming down, he patted the Desert Eagle he wore in his holster, and added, "But they do make extremely effective weapons."

For hours the military display continued.

Wave after wave of tanks rolled by the stand, followed by armored vehicles that could traverse almost any terrain.

As uniformed waiters passed glasses of champagne to his guests, the colonel made a sign, and the sound of a dozen jets exploded overhead as the aircraft dipped and twisted to show off the skill of their pilots.

A banker from India asked a question. "Will Captain Khalid lead them?"

"No. He is busy elsewhere," the colonel replied smoothly, then glanced at Dr. Nis to see his reaction, but the scientist merely nodded and said nothing.

"The parade was impressive," the banker from South Africa commented.

"It should be," Saddam replied. "I used the money all of you have advanced against our oil to pay for it."

Something occurred to Saddam, and with a pleasant smile he asked, "Would you like to see a demonstration of how we are going to put the soldiers of our neighbors out of action?"

Hans Zeibart looked at the others in his group. None of them looked happy at the suggestion. "I think we can assume your men are effective," the Swiss banker said.

The colonel thought about the culling-out process the soldiers had gone through to remain among the living. "Very."

"Which brings me to a delicate subject," the Japanese banker said. "The question of repayment of our consortium's loans."

The Swiss banker saw the hint of irritation in the Arab leader's expression. "I think we can postpone that subject until our meeting tomorrow evening," he said quickly.

Saddam stood and clapped his hands. At his gesture nine beautiful young women entered the reviewing stand and moved to his side.

He smiled at them. They were the finest his ambassadors could recruit for the occasion, and ostensibly they were companions who would entertain and amuse the important guests.

"Choose your companions, gentlemen," he suggested.

The six guests surveyed their options, unable to mask the bright light of lust in their eyes.

A redhead from Rome. Three light blondes, one from London and the two other from Los Angeles. A brunette from Barcelona, and two from Latin America. A young girl from Thailand, no more than fourteen, stood shyly in line with the others. Next to her, a gold-trimmed sari covering her hair, was a dark-skinned beauty from Bombay.

As the men smilingly made their choices, Saddam leaned over to Randall Manderill, the American banker. "For you, I have found a beautiful young man from Paris," he whispered.

With a well-pleased expression, the New Yorker nodded.

AS HE WATCHED the six men leave, five with companions on their arms, the colonel turned to the blond man next to him.

"It has been a successful day."

"Your guests seemed pleased," Nis commented.

Saddam hated that he could never guess what the scientist was thinking or feeling.

"And you?"

Nis shrugged. "I'll be happy when the goal has been achieved."

He gave the colonel a reassuring glance, letting the man think their goals were the same. But what he needed, Nis thought, glancing at the faint tremor in his hands, was energy, the stuff of life.

31

Hogan had been checking the engine under the hood of the jeep when he sensed human presence. Quickly he straightened and reached for his CAR-15.

Two dozen hard-faced men were staring at him. Each of them held an automatic rifle in his hands, aimed at the American's chest and ready to fire.

Black Jack didn't think they were Saddam's men. The color of their turbans was different.

These looked like bandits. Hogan knew the Middle Eastern countries were plagued with bandits who raided villages and hid in the mountains.

He briefly wondered where Brom was. He had a knack of showing up with his howling sword when Hogan was in trouble.

"You," the tall, flint-faced leader of the men, said in broken English, shoving the muzzle of his M-16 into Black Jack's chest. "Are you responsible for the slaughter on the hill?"

"No, I didn't kill the sheep. Soldiers did."

"Saddam's pigs?"

"Yes."

"We found their bodies," the man said coldly. "You killed them?"

There was no point in lying. "Yes, I killed them."

The flint-faced man turned to the others. "This is the warrior who killed the pigs," he shouted in Arabic, and suddenly the hard expressions turned into smiles.

"Good. There should have been more of them for you to kill." He backed away and allowed the American more room.

"I am called Yakut. How are you called?"

"Hogan," the American said, extending his hand.

Yakut, who was obviously the leader of the troop, slapped it with his open palm and laughed. "You are American. Here we do not shake hands."

"The soldiers killed a little girl," Black Jack said.

The expression on Yakut's face became mournful. "I know. We found her body. And that of her dog. You put her in front of the shrine?"

"I didn't know what else to do."

"She was not Yazidi. She was a Kurd," the leader of the men said coldly. Then softened his tone. "But it is all right. God is god even if it is the wrong one."

Meanwhile several of the other men were starting a small fire, and in a while the smell of roasting meat was wafting in the air.

Yakut saw Hogan cast an appraising glance at the food.

"Come, we eat together like brothers."

As Black Jack sat around the fire and shared their meal, Yakut explained their presence. "We are Kurds, the fiercest of the fierce."

Several of the other men nodded in agreement before turning back to their food.

"Once we had our own land, Kurdistan. Then foreign armies came and stole it from us. Some gave us a little in return. Not enough, but at least they wanted peace with the Kurds. But not Saddam. He is not a man. He is a mad dog who should be killed like all mad dogs. He has enslaved all the people in this country."

"But not us," somebody shouted.

"Right," Yakut agreed. "Not the Kurds. We are free men, and not even Saddam can turn us into mindless animals like he has everybody else."

"How can the handful of you beat him?"

"Throughout this land, there are thousands." He paused to make a point. "Many, many thousands just like us. We hide in the mountains and in the villages and wait for the right moment to rise up against the mad dog and his soldiers."

Suddenly Yakut stopped and stared at Hogan. "And why are you here?"

"For the same reason. To stop Saddam."

"One man?"

Black Jack smiled quietly. "Sometimes one man can do more than a whole army."

The Kurd leader nodded. "True. Look at how the Prophet, blessed be his name, changed the world. How will you do your work?"

Hogan hesitated, uncertain about sharing information concerning his mission, then decided to take a chance. "Saddam has a chemical plant in Qatir, and he plans to invade the countries around him."

"We know about both," Yakut replied. "We have heard of the poisons he has made in his factory. And we have watched his troops practice secretly how to kill in preparation for the war."

"Without the plant or Saddam, there will be no war," the American said.

"Good," Yakut shouted gleefully, slapping Hogan on the back. "We have lots of hand grenades we have stolen from Saddam's own military supplies. We will help you blow it up."

The rest of the irregular troop raised their weapons in the air and shouted their agreement lustily.

Hogan and Yakut got to their feet quickly, ready to break camp.

"Before we go," the Kurd leader said, "I have one question." He looked at the krall in Black Jack's waistband. "How did you cut off the head of the pig of a soldier with just a knife?"

32

It was obvious the conference had been successful. Each of the guests had a companion at his side, including the American banker, who passed off the young man with him as an interpreter.

Judging by the warm attention and glances full of promise, the bankers' companions were determined to please at any cost. A flirtatious getting-acquainted mood pervaded the sumptuous table, overshadowing the wonderful assortment of fancy appetizers, main courses and the endless array of delectable sweets.

Food had also been sent to the crews of the six jets who waited at the airfield next to the palace to transport the bankers back to their homes.

Even Dr. Nis seemed pleased at last, Saddam thought, looking at the expression on his scientific adviser's face.

It was time for a toast.

Standing up, he lifted a glass filled with bottled water. "I propose a toast."

The others turned away from their companions and looked at the colonel.

He waved his glass aloft at his guests. "To our honored guests, who have shown their faith in the success of our mission with the one thing they love most—money...."

The bankers laughed easily, knowing they were on the verge of making a lot more money.

"To the scientist who helped make this all possible..." Saddam turned and nodded at the blond man. "And to our agents, who are at this very moment crossing the borders into the neighboring countries to prepare the way for our brave soldiers, so the holy campaign will start off so much more smoothly.''

Everybody around the table picked up their glasses and joined in the toast.

Hans Zeibart beamed at Saddam. "And when do the soldiers make the actual crossings?"

The impeccably dressed colonel wagged a finger at him. "That, my dear friend, is classified information—" He paused for effect, then added with a broad smile, "But it is safe to tell you it will happen within twenty-four hours."

"Good, good," the dapper financier said approvingly. "How long do you estimate the campaign will take?"

"No more than two weeks. Perhaps less, thanks to Dr. Nis."

The bankers around the long table turned to the enigmatic-looking doctor and applauded him.

Nis nodded and smiled, lifting an indolent hand in acknowledgement. And right after that, he thought to himself, shipments of the drug will go out to the various uranium-mining sites so I can begin *my* campaign. He looked at the shiny-faced celebrants, at the little men with little, finite plans.

THE SIX MEN slipped across the border ten miles south of the border post and moved stealthily until they reached the outskirts of the small border village of Rayamadi.

"The well is at the far end," one of them whispered, adjusting the heavy leather bag he carried on his shoulder.

Leading the way, he moved past the darkened huts, then paused when he heard the braying of a horse.

"No one suspects we are here," a second man said in low tones.

"The colonel has given us many places to visit before morning. Let us not waste too much time here."

The lead man nodded and resumed his movement toward the stone wall that surrounded the water supply.

When the six of them had reached the well, he slipped the bag from his shoulder and reached inside for two of the vials he had been given.

"If our other teams are as successful, by next week we will be given a share of the wealth of these villages," he predicted.

Suddenly a barrage of gunfire from every direction suspended all further conversation, and the six men died an instantaneous death.

A group of uniformed soldiers rushed to them and checked each body. The sergeant who was in charge plucked the two vials from the dead man's hand, then turned to another soldier whose radio-telephone unit hung suspended from his shoulder.

"Send a message off saying we found them in plenty of time."

33

The city of Qatir sat on a sunbaked plateau in the center of the country. All around it was the desert. Not the soft sands of the Sahara, but crusted land covered with a thin layer of loose dry soil that whirled at the whim of the wind.

The city itself had been built on an ancient oasis. A network of wells and underground viaducts constructed by an ancient civilization provided life-sustaining water.

The old city, a mosaic of crumbling, aged structures and bazaars, sat at the junction of three large roads that had once been caravan routes. A mile away, behind high stone walls and massive wooden gates, was the ruler's palace and its gardens. Set in the middle of several acres of carefully tended parks, the immaculately maintained structure stood imperiously apart from the shabby dwellings of the majority of the people.

What had once been the harem had been converted to a guest house for honored visitors of the ruler. Like the palace, it was safely hidden behind the protective walls.

Just behind the impressive complex was a small airfield, with runways long enough to accommodate medium-sized jets.

Its silhouette visible in the distance, far away from the city or the palace, was the chemical plant, its tall stacks belching a yellow-looking smoke into the sky. A tall, electrified cyclone fence protected it, along with a small force of armed guards.

From a rise that overlooked the city, Hogan lay on his belly on the ground next to Yakut and carefully studied the surrounding area through his night-vision binoculars.

Everything was exactly where the southerner said they would be. Yakut had confirmed the accuracy of Wilson's information when the two of them went over the map Black Jack had with him.

The only surprise had been the half-dozen jets parked on the fields. From their markings, their home bases were Zurich, Tokyo, London, Johannesburg, New Delhi and New York.

Khalid's notes had mentioned the backing provided by foreign bankers for Saddam's plans. They must have come to hold a meeting of the board of directors, Hogan decided.

He wondered if he should delay his next move until they had left. Then he remembered the dead children and the photographs.

What was it Wilson had said? Officially the government couldn't go after them. But he wasn't official. In fact, Hogan remembered with a smile, he didn't even exist.

The Kurdish leader's question interrupted his thoughts. "What is it you want from us?"

"I plan to break into the chemical plant after midnight—" he checked his watch "—two hours from now. If you can create a diversion that will draw the guards around the complex, I can slip in through the front gates."

"Easily done," Yakut promised with a smile. "And then what?"

"And then, when you see me come out, run like hell."

Yakut saluted him and got up and wandered down to where the rest of his men were waiting. Hogan looked after him thoughtfully, then took out his krall and looked at its shiny length. Suddenly he saw, as in a mirror or a screen, twin moons veiled by clouds and a strange city....

A SMALL SECONDARY gate to the city of Tella swung open. Six black-painted figures slipped out and moved across the plains toward the Kalabrian camp, clutching long knives in their hands.

When they reached the camp, they waited until the two guards had turned their backs, then moved quietly behind them and slit their throats with their knives as they muffled the moans of the dying men with their hands.

Crouching, they looked around the vast camp. In the distance one of them saw a tall spear on which was mounted a pennant with the green, red and yellow colors of the Kalabrian army.

"The pennant is always flown wherever the Lord Brom sleeps," one of them said in a fierce whisper, and the small group moved with stealth past the rows of sleeping bodies.

DRAKA TRIED to sleep, but the thoughts in his mind kept pounding away at him. Traitor, a voice inside charged. Murderer, a second voice accused. Except for the stain it would leave on his innocent son's reputation, he was tempted to ram the short sword he gripped in his right hand into his stomach and gladly let the life fluid run out of him.

The bright, shining future the queen had promised him had become tarnished. To rule the kingdom of his dead brother had been his dream since childhood. He'd even killed his brother and his brother's wife to realize it. Now the only thing he was grateful for was that Mondlock had convinced his only child, Sola, to travel to the city of Leanad, where he could learn the secrets of the Knowers.

It was impossible to sleep with the burden he carried, he decided, and sat up. Then he saw them.

Six figures, stooped low, moving quickly through the sleeping ranks. He glanced over his shoulder. They were heading for Brom.

Jumping to his feet, he rushed at them with his raised sword. Slashing at the chest of the first one, he felt his weapon slice across the breastbone beneath the skin. With a muted grunt, the would-be assailant slid to the ground.

Turning to face the other five, Draka poised for a second charge, then felt the point of a dagger slice across his neck.

He tried to call for assistance, but no sound came out. He put his hand to his windpipe. It had been severed.

Two of the painted invaders grabbed him while a third ran a knife into his chest and twisted the blade with a sharp wrench of his wrist.

Staring with muted surprise, the elderly man died suspended on the knife.

Easing the body to the ground, the assailant wiped the blood from his blade and followed the other four toward the sleeping form of the Kalabrian leader.

BROM HAD BEEN DREAMING of the shimmering cloud that sent him on his journeys to and from his twin. He was startled awake to the sound of loud explosions. Grabbing his krall, he opened his eyes and saw the twisted sneer on the painted face staring down at him. The battle-ax locked in the man's hand was slashing down.

Shoving a booted foot at the attacker's crotch, Brom shoved the surprised antagonist backward onto his back, then threw himself on top of him. Ramming his blade deep into the fallen man's chest, he ignored the gasping cries and shoved the knife deeper until a fountain of blood spurted up at him.

Jumping to his feet, the red-bearded hellion heard a second series of explosions and spun around to see the source.

Hogan, his feet planted wide, was gripping a fire-stick and spraying four bodies on the ground with searing metal.

Satisfied that the assassins were dead, Black Jack ceased firing and looked at the bearded Kalabrian. "Maybe you should think about giving up sleep for a while," he said calmly.

Brom nodded, then glanced at the krall Hogan was wearing.

"You didn't use the gift," he commented.

"I will." He looked around. "What's going on?"

The Kalabrian told him the plan of attack, then remembered something. "Zhuzak did say you would come if we needed you."

Hogan looked surprised. "The wrestler said that?"

A new voice joined theirs. "Yes, I, the wrestler, said that."

The American glanced to his right. The massive warrior he had fought was next to him. Hogan nodded, wondering what the Kalabrian officer would do next.

He didn't have to wait long to find out. Zhuzak wrapped his huge arms around Black Jack's midsection and squeezed.

"It's good to see you, *Dula*. I look forward to wrestling you again."

Still feeling the soreness in his ribs from their last encounter, Hogan shook his head. "My bones don't."

While the wrestling champion laughed, a grim-faced commander came up to Brom. "Your uncle has been killed," he said quietly.

"Assassinated by the intruders?"

The man nodded. "But not before he took one of them with him."

The flame-haired Kalabrian bowed his head and offered a sad epitaph. "Whatever was worrying Draka will never concern him again. He died a warrior."

Then he led the way to the body to gaze at the features of his uncle and thus pay his last respects. Only Hogan didn't follow, and the next moment he was nowhere to be seen....

34

The American warrior had made a quick stop at the airfield next to the palace before heading for the chemical plant.

Now he drove his vehicle around the perimeter of the city to avoid running into soldiers. He skipped the roads and ran the jeep through the bumpy rises and gullies of the desert until he saw the huge factory loom in front of him.

For a military dictatorship, security was unusually lax, he thought as he parked the vehicle on the outside of the high cyclone fence. He saw the thin electrical wires running across the top perimeter of the chain-link structure; they would trigger an alarm if anyone tried cutting into the fence.

Behind the fence he could hear the muffled growls of guard dogs. A pair of armed, uniformed men led two angry-looking rottweilers on chains and kept looking around as they walked the exterior of the plant.

According to the German architect's plans Wilson had supplied, there were only two ways to get in or out of Qatir Chemicals. One was through the main gate, and the other was through a wider gate through which the workers came and left and all deliveries and shipments passed. Both were heavily guarded by armed men.

Opening one of the bags, Hogan loaded his pockets with plastic explosives and timers, then grabbed his assault rifle and moved around the fence and waited in the shadows.

The diversion that came minutes later was more like a Fourth of July celebration than an attack.

Two dozen horsemen stormed around the outside of the complex, throwing lighted sticks of dynamite in every direction. The barrage of explosions alerted the company of soldiers Saddam had stationed at the plant to protect it from intruders.

Soon a dozen armored vehicles were chasing the horsemen along the road that led through the desert. As they galloped into the dark night, the Kurds kept tossing dynamite behind them.

Under cover of the confusion, Hogan darted through the courtyard beyond the fence. A couple of armed guards who had not joined the pursuit sent hot lead his way, but the American triggered two rounds from his assault rifle. The hollowpoints tore apart the stunned soldiers' bodies, and the next moment Hogan had already sprinted inside the entryway.

With his back to the wall, he quickly moved along a hallway, then pushed open a pair of swinging doors at its end. The blueprints had indicated that he should be in an area where finished products were held for shipment.

Pausing briefly, he set a timer and planted an explosive package. The timers were all to be set for thirty minutes. He had to accomplish everything before then if he didn't want to have another confrontation with the devil.

Hogan checked inside the shipping-holding area, and it looked devoid of life, but suddenly he heard loud scuffling from behind the swinging doors. He flattened himself against the wall, his weapon held in readiness.

The doors swung violently open, and a trio of men burst into the room, their automatic weapons instantly blazing.

Hogan put them in his sights and washed them with a continuous spray of death. As they crumpled to the floor, Hogan turned to the cardboard cases that were neatly stacked throughout the vast area. Tearing one open, he grabbed a handful of vials and shoved them in his pocket.

Back in the main corridor, he set three more timed explosive packages and placed them strategically for maximum effect.

From behind a wider pair of doors, he could hear the steady hum of machinery. The manufacturing area.

He pushed open the doors and stopped to search for armed trouble, but saw no one except a dozen workers in white lab coats.

Firing a burst at the ceiling, he watched their faces turn pale as they jerked around from their task and saw him.

"Get out," he yelled, waving his gun at them.

They didn't understand his words, but they understood the meaning of his gesture. As if chased by the devil, they ran screaming from the area.

There were two places left to check. He tried to picture the plans for the plant. Raw materials were stored at the other end of the building.

Moving quickly through the huge factory, he kept watching for opposition. Two angry soldiers charged at him from the shelter of an intersecting corridor. One of them lobbed a grenade, and the deadly egg came sailing through the air.

With a backward roll, Black Jack fell behind the cover of a huge processing machine just as the fragmentation bomb exploded. He waited until the two uniformed men moved forward to search for his body, then rose and freed a short burst at them.

The men became nothing more than tattered bits of flesh and bone. Running over the suddenly blood-slickened floor, the American broke into a sprint. He had less than twelve minutes left to fulfill his objectives.

The storage area was housed behind a locked chain-link fence. Hogan had no time to try to pick the complex lock. Jerking the pin from a 40 mm fragmentation grenade, he rolled it at the fence, then threw himself inside a nearby janitor's closet.

The reverberating blast shook the walls of his hiding place. When he emerged, the gate was swinging open.

Quickly he armed another package and tossed it under a tall tank marked Highly Explosive.

He took a moment to check his wristwatch. Ten minutes.

Getting back to the front lobby of the building at breakneck speed, he took the steps two at a time. The plans called for the executive offices to be located at the near end of the second floor.

He found a door marked Doctor Nis. It was locked, and he shot the lock off with a 2-shot burst.

Then he heard the click of weapons behind him, and a voice shouted, "Drop your weapon and raise your hands!"

As he turned, he saw two grim-looking soldiers. He dropped the rifle and started to lift his hands when he saw a swirling hint of shimmering to his left.

Brom was standing there, legs spread, gripping the assault rifle Black Jack had given him. Puzzled at Hogan's fixed stare, one of the guards turned his head to follow the line of vision.

The Kalabrian squeezed the trigger. A continuous burst of burning lead tore into the two guards and wall.

"Enough," Hogan shouted.

Brom reluctantly took his finger off the trigger.

"That was overkill," the American remarked as he picked up his weapon.

At the bearded warrior's puzzled expression, Hogan said, "I'll explain later."

"I'll expect an explanation," the Kalabrian replied, then there was a faint shimmering around him and the next moment he was gone. Hogan rubbed his eyes. This kind of thing still took him by surprise.

Hogan shoved the door to Nis's office open and rushed in.

It was empty. A quick search through the drawers and cabinets revealed nothing, and it looked as if nobody had ever occupied the room. But it wasn't the time to worry if Nis was hiding in the plant. Time had almost run out.

As he dashed down the stairs, he literally ran into an armed soldier who was screaming to the skies for his god to save him. The hysterical guard saw Hogan and started shrieking. "Shaitan has come!"

There was no time for Black Jack to clear up the misunderstanding. He had to get out of the plant immediately.

The crazed man grabbed Hogan's wrist and refused to let go.

The American pulled the krall from its scabbard and drove it into the other man's abdomen. He'd have more time to feel bad about this later.

"Shaitan has killed me," the dying soldier cried out as he fell to the floor, still clutching Black Jack's wrist.

Hogan pulled his hand free and took off at top speed to get out of the building and through the main gate.

Diving into the jeep, he jammed the gas pedal and went from zero to sixty miles per hour in seconds.

He kept the pedal to the floor until the huge, blinding burst of searing energy from behind him shoved the vehicle fifty feet forward.

Night had become day as towers of flames roared into the sky from every corner of the plant. A thousand screaming birds were a faint whisper compared to the raging sounds from what had once been a huge factory. Massive columns of smoke drifted upward, born of the crackling of the chemical-fed flames.

As a downswirl of smoke reached his nose, Black Jack made a face and started driving. He had one more thing he had to do before he could assist Brom. He had to find Nis.

He glanced at his rearview mirror, and his eyes widened at the strange, dreamlike scene he saw reflected in it....

BROM RODE at the front of his troops as they moved against the walled city. Zhuzak, who had been appointed temporary senior commander, moved his horse to the bearded man's side.

"We don't have the battering rams and other devices to help us break into the city. Even if we did, we will lose a lot of men trying to capture it," he warned.

"Then we must all die," the Kalabrian leader replied firmly.

As the burly captain turned and moved his mount back to the other commanders, Brom kept looking around for any sign that his twin soulbrother from the other world had returned. Perhaps Hogan would have some magic to help them. Brom hoped so.

In front of them, the main gates to Tella opened, and a horde of black-painted soldiers poured out onto the plains. This time, instead of attacking, they waited in tense silence.

Even from this distance, Brom could see the lust and anticipation of slaughter in their faces.

THE BANKERS FLED from the guest quarters in the palace, their faces filled with horror at the flames pouring into the sky from across the city. Their pilots had been torn away from their pursuits of pleasure and were only feet ahead of them.

From the edge of the old city, Hogan watched through his night-vision binoculars the terrified men, running and trying to get their clothes on at the same time. These were the men who were willing to let Saddam carry out his scheme of conquest—a scheme that would visit horrible deaths on thousands of innocents.

He felt no guilt about the stop he'd made at the airfield earlier as he watched them run into their planes. While the pilots started the engines, Black Jack glanced behind him at the now-lighter bags on the back seat. Everything he had requested had come in handy.

He started the motor and drove the jeep toward the palace.

THE BUSINESS JETS began to taxi down the runway. One at a time they gracefully lifted from the ground and climbed into the air. Six jets all running to escape the nightmare.

Suddenly a series of sun-bright explosions in the sky lit the Qatir night. A shower of metal debris showered down on the airfield.

Standing alone at the edge of the airfield, Saddam stared in stunned horror at the bits of what once had been the private planes of powerful rich men. Now they, and everything else, were gone.

He felt the muzzle of a gun pressing in his back. Terrified, he stuttered the question. "What do you want?"

"Nis."

"I don't know where he is."

Hogan didn't have time to play games. He had a promise to keep. He looked down at the canvas bag of supplies on the ground next to him and moved his Colt Commander to the officer's neck.

"When the explosions from the chemical plant started, I ran out to see what happened. When I returned, he was gone."

"Who is he? Where is he from?"

The colonel's voice began to quaver. "I don't know. He comes and goes like the wind."

"Or the devil."

Saddam half turned his head as he tried to regain his commanding manner and voice. "I was shocked to see all my guests' planes explode.... I demand you tell me who you are—and in whose service. You won't be able to get far...my men are everywhere...."

Black Jack pulled the trigger as he replied, "You are competition for the devil, and he sent me to take you out."

When Saddam lay still on the ground, Hogan quickly worked out a plan in his mind. He needed to stock up on a few items of war, because he knew there was someplace his help was desperately needed.

Just wait until you see the look on Brom's face when he sees the goodies he'll be getting, Hogan told himself as he left the scene of carnage in a hurry.

35

"Wait up for me."

Brom recognized the voice. He turned and saw Hogan riding toward him on a mount that Brom recognized as Draka's horse. There was a huge cloth sack tied to the saddle behind him.

"What do you carry in the sack?"

Black Jack smiled. "The queen's worst nightmare."

The Kalabrian warrior saw the battle sword and krall Hogan wore in his belt, near a gun and strange metal balls.

"I see you still have my gift. Where did you find the sword?"

"Near the horse," the American replied.

Draka must have lost the weapon in the fight, Brom concluded, and changed the subject. "As you can see, we are in a fix," he admitted.

Hogan nodded. He opened the large canvas bag behind him and took out the CAR-15. "But I have brought some other toys with me—and they may help."

"I do not respect how you handle the steel," Brom said, "but some of your magic tricks would be useful, I admit." He pointed to the fearsome black horde and their officers waiting for them in front of the city walls. "That's what we have to deal with—each crazed one is like ten. We must destroy them before we find a way to break down the doors and enter Tella. Have you any suggestions?"

The American smiled at the redheaded warrior. "How good are you at pitching?"

When Brom looked puzzled, Hogan tried another approach.

"Have you ever thrown a stone a long distance?"

"In the games, I have often won the stone-throwing contest."

"Good." Black Jack reached into the bag and handed the Kalabrian a fragmentation grenade. "When I tell you, pull on the circle, count to five and throw one of these at the enemy troops. But don't keep the deadly grenade in your hand once you'd pulled on that tab and counted to five—or it will tear you apart like a thousand demons."

Brom was skeptical. "What can this small metal stone do?"

"Try it. You'll like it," Hogan promised, shoving his assault rifle into the saddle.

Spurring their horses, the two warriors raced to the front of the Kalabrian troops and continued until they were fifty yards from where Raikana's forces were waiting.

At the sight of Brom's fierce red head, the enemy officers shouted for their men to charge.

"Now," Hogan shouted as he ripped a fragmentation grenade from his webbed belt, pulled out the pin and spiraled it at the oncoming attackers.

Brom went through the same motions, having watched closely, and suddenly twelve mindless ones exploded into bits of flesh and blood as the ground around them erupted. The shocked troops didn't move, frightened that the earthquake would come again.

Black Jack tossed another grenade to Brom.

"Let's do it again," he yelled as he grabbed another for himself, armed it and spiraled it at a selected cluster of black-painted barbarians.

Brom was not to be outdone, and at least twenty of the enemy screamed in mortal agony as hot metal fragments tore into their bodies. Hundreds more began to shriek in fear, then turned in panic to run from the death throwers.

The commanders who tried to stop them were trampled by the stampede of terrified foot soldiers, who dropped their weapons in their haste to escape destruction.

Panic became pandemonium as more than two thousand black-painted men joined in the frenzied exodus.

Hogan accelerated the reaction by pitching two more fragmentation grenades at the fleeing forces.

Brom turned to his troops. "After them!" he shouted.

The waiting Kalabrian army charged after the deserting savages. Soon the rolling hills outside the walled city of Tella became a sea of slaughter as the warriors engaged in hand-to-hand combat.

Hundreds of fountains of blood spurted from the fallen bodies as warriors vented their revenge for murdered wives, children and friends on the hysterical barbarians.

Brom and Hogan watched the frightful scene for a while, then shifted their attention to the massive doors that prevented access to the city.

"My men will have to scale the walls and open them from inside," the Kalabrian decided.

"Let's try my way first," Hogan suggested.

He led the others to the wall, dismounted and ran to the gate. The flame-haired Kalabrian joined him.

Hogan handed his assault rifle over and pointed to the parapet on top of the wall. "Play bodyguard while I do my thing," he said, then noticed the puzzled expression on Brom's face.

He'd forgotten. Slang didn't work here.

"Make sure no one stops me," Hogan said to clarify things, and this time the Kalabrian nodded.

Hogan crouchwalked to the doors and planted explosives, then set the timers. He started to run back, then veered back and planted several more in the ground next to the walls on either side of the gate.

As he dashed back to his mount, Brom was spraying the wall behind him with slugs. He turned and saw an archer tumble to the ground.

"Nice shooting," he shouted as he got on his horse. "Now let's get out of here."

The two of them took off in a furious gallop from the city walls. But even the thunderous beat of the horses' hooves couldn't mask the series of booming explosions that made the scream of the Sjarik at its worst a tame whisper by comparison.

They reined in their horses and turned back.

Where wood and solid stone had stood to prevent unwanted entrance to Tella, there was only a gaping opening and rubble.

Brom rose in his saddle and whirled his huge sword over his head until the air filled with a howling sound. Kalabrian warriors turned and stared in his direction, and he pointed his sword at the breach in the city walls and spurred his horse toward it.

After retrieving two more fragmentation grenades from the bag tied to his saddle, Hogan joined the invasion.

As the Kalabrian troops moved into the city, Brom sensed that Raikana was still a power to contend with. She still had enough men who were ready to kill for her, to die for her. He could feel their hidden presence as he led his warriors into the large open square at the entrance to Tella.

He had not been in his birthplace for more than a year, he realized as he looked around. What had been his family's home for a thousand years was only a pile of structures and timber that had been witness to abominations.

Sitting on his horse, he glanced at the towers of the palace that rose above the city and recalled the happy memories of childhood. But only memories. What he would have considered unthinkable as a child, he would now have to do as a conqueror.

"Put the torch to the city," he proclaimed to the officers who waited for his orders.

Hogan moved to his side. "Let me start it."

Brom looked around. "There is a lot to be burned, Hogan."

Black Jack nodded, then pulled off one of the incendiary grenades on his belt and rode to the open doorway of a building. He shouted inside, then dashed in and saw it was empty. When he emerged again, he pulled the pin, tossed the metal egg inside, then rode back to where the Kalabrian leader was waiting.

An explosion of flame leaped out from every opening of the building as the grenade detonated. A raging fire began to consume the structure to the amazement of the gathered officers.

Hogan glanced at the bearded leader. "Next stop?"

As Brom and Hogan paused at the palace gates, they looked behind them. The city was wallowing in flames. Below them they could hear the curses of soldiers as they fought with pockets of the hiding desperate Jaddueii.

"Perhaps they once were men," Brom said grimly. "But they are not anymore. Now they are vermin who will contaminate if left to live."

He faced the palace gates, looking serious and sad. "This has been our home since the history of Kalabria began. How much blood has been shed just so we can get it back."

Hogan understood how he felt. "This isn't about a palace. This is about people."

He thought back to his own impossible dreams of having home, a wife and children. But he knew that fate had decreed otherwise.

"When the smell of cooking and the laughing of children fill the streets of Tella, you will know why you fought this war."

Brom nodded. "You are a wise man, Hogan." Then he
added, "Let us go inside and clean this place."

Hogan wasn't sure how wise he was. But the Kalabrian
was right about one thing. They still had a palace to get
back.

They dismounted and entered the palace on foot. Brom
gripped his sword and krall in his hands. Hogan set the
sword aside and rested his finger against the trigger of his
CAR-15 as they carefully checked the halls off the main entry.

"Everyone has fled," the bearded man announced.

"Let's make sure," the American replied, and rolled a
fragmentation grenade into a large reception room.

Pulling Brom and himself to the floor, he waited until he
heard the small missile vent its metal-splintered fury.

Helping the Kalabrian to his feet, he shook his head and
commented, "Maybe you're right about everyone taking
powder."

Brom had been wrong. One of the Jaddueii had hidden
behind a pillar at the top of the stairs. He stepped forward
and poised his lance to fling at the strangely dressed warrior below him, but an instinct warned the flame-haired
Kalabrian, and he looked up. Swiftly Brom threw his krall,
and the flat side of the blade dealt a glancing blow to the
assassin's head and momentarily stunned him.

Hogan pointed his weapon up and washed the upper
landing with molten lead, then cautiously led the way up the
stairs.

Brom retrieved his knife, and they went through to the
inner sanctums of the palace.

BROM AND HOGAN SIZED UP the doors leading to what used
to be the royal suite, then together they rammed their
shoulders against the wooden doors and forced them open.

Six women in black were sprawled around a large stone
statue of Raik.

Brom looked at the prone women, then leaned down and lifted their eyelids, one by one. They were clearly dead, probably from some swallowed poison.

"Kalabria will be reclaimed—even from the memory of such evils. They will merely be reminders to honor the right and true way," Brom said in low tones. "But we still have to find Raikana."

CUJA HAD BEEN APPOINTED personal protector by Raikana just recently. He felt honored and was determined to fight to the last. He had gathered the remnants of his small force outside the queen's bedroom. Just beyond them, past the corner, were the stairs leading to it, an access they had to defend if they were to make a stand.

"Let nobody get in, or you will account to me," he warned.

They heard the sounds of men dashing up the stairs. The new captain directed, "Wait until they come into view before you attack."

Cuja took a furtive look and recognized the red beard of one of them. He'd overheard the queen curse that very man's existence often enough.

"Now," he shouted, and led the charge.

"My turn," Black Jack said as he braced the CAR-15 and began to pepper the air with body-seeking hollowpoints.

The stunned attackers fell over, overwhelmed by the sound and by the fact that death sought them out as though by magic.

Cuja stared in shock at the wholesale destruction and started to flee down a corridor, but Brom was right at his heels.

Cornered, the queen's captain turned and lashed his sword at the fierce and righteously angry warrior. Brom easily sidestepped the move and gripped his howling sword tightly. His blow, when it whistled through the air, cut through Cuja's torso in one stroke.

Stunned by the death blow, Cuja looked down at h[...] carved torso, then with a curse crumpled to the bloo[...] stained floor.

RAIKANA PACED the floor nervously. There was a hidde[...] passage behind the fireplace in the bedroom. She cou[...] easily escape through it, but where would she go?

The solution was simple. Back to Tana. There were troop[...] loyal to her waiting there. All she had to do was find [...] mount and slip out of the city.

"No," a voice said quietly.

She whirled around and saw Nis, the magician. She wasn[...] terribly surprised to see him appear, even though the cit[...] was in shambles and death walked its streets. Nis had va[...] powers and seemed to have commanded things to bend t[...] his will.

"No?" She looked puzzled.

"There is no escape. You have failed," he said in a fla[...] calm voice.

"I can gather new troops," she said, plucking at h[...] sleeve with bejeweled fingers. "Together we can return an[...] conquer Kalabria."

Nis shook his head, turned around, took a few steps an[...] faded into thin air.

But Raikana could still hear his voice in her head.

"No. I am the queen. I only do what I want," she wail[...] at the empty room.

As she continued to argue, she reached for the knife s[...] kept at her bedside and plunged it into her heart.

THE TWIN WARRIORS stood on the threshold of the magni[...] icently appointed bedchamber and saw the body of the r[...] ven-haired woman sprawled across the bed.

Brom moved closer and spat at her body. "My paren[...] conceived me in that bed," he said bitterly. "But she wasn[...] acting alone. She may have been mad, filled with evil spi[...]

its, but I think the magician was behind her plans. Let's find him."

They searched through the palace for the magician. Finally they located the door to his sanctum and rammed it open with their shoulders. They found it in shambles, with broken glass everywhere and rivers of spilled chemicals.

But no magician.

They looked at each other wordlessly, and finally Brom broke the silence. "Is he dead?"

They both felt the presence in the room as they heard a voice in their heads.

"No. I cannot die."

Stunned, the American looked at the Kalabrian. "Did you hear that?"

Brom nodded, then stared at the empty air in front of him and asked, "Who are you?"

"I do not need a name. I know who I am."

"Okay," Black Jack said. "Then what are you?"

"I am energy. The rarest kind of energy that carries with it intelligence."

Brom wondered what kind of god was talking to them. "Why are you here?"

"To find for that which is useful only to me. And then, to bring beautiful order ... which you can't even begin to understand."

The rage in both warriors at the senseless destruction in their worlds began to build within them.

Hogan spoke up, his voice sharp with anger. "What about all the people who've suffered because of you?"

"Suffered? What does the word mean?"

Brom and Black Jack could sense a hesitancy. Then the voice in their heads continued.

"The sooner I find what I seek, the sooner I leave your worlds alone. Will you help?"

The warriors had the same initial reaction. To help might mean that whoever it was that talking in their heads would then leave their worlds.

Hogan remembered Nis. He called out a question. "Does Nis work for you?"

"Nis is me."

The warriors heard the reply and, almost in unison, gave their answer.

"N-o-o-o-o!"

The presence in the room was no more, like a cold draft that stops when the window is closed. Brom and Hogan exchanged a disbelieving glance. "Was it a trick of the magician?" Brom asked.

"Maybe. Whoever it was, I think he was lying about being indestructible. There's got to be a way to destroy him."

Brom looked thoughtful. "But what is it?"

The American shook his head. "I don't know. But I have a feeling that there has got to be a way, and I am as certain of that as I am of the fact that Nis will be back. We haven't seen the last of him, my friend."

THE CITY FLICKERED EERILY in the evening light as some of its quarters continued to burn.

Brom and Hogan watched the smoky scene of a deadly battle in silence. Then Black Jack turned to the Kalabrian leader. "What now?"

"Most of the troops will stay here. I will ride back with some of my right-hand men and begin the task of rebuilding Kalabria, reclaiming it from the ruins it has been brought to by Raikana."

"A good plan, my friend, and a noble one."

"And you?"

Hogan was surprised at the question. "What about me?"

"Where do you go now?"

The American shrugged. "Home, I suppose," but he didn't sound very enthusiastic.

"Why not stay here and help us?"

He remembered what he had told the girl with the wild strawberry-colored hair.

"This is not my home."

"Many will miss you."

"Does that mean you?"

"And a temple girl," Brom added with an encouraging wink. Hogan smiled, but he knew it was time to go back and find out if Wilson had gotten his radioed message. And see what new lessons Mok Seng would insist on teaching.

Still, it was tempting. "I'll miss both of you," he said, then added, "But there will be another time."

Brom grasped his shoulder with a powerful hand and looked into his eyes.

"Yes, my friend, I am sure there will be another time."

EPILOGUE

Hogan and Mok Seng wandered silently through the tiny garden the two of them had painstakingly created behind the temple.

"You are quiet for a change," the tiny monk observed. "Are you recovered from your mission?"

"Sure. Just a few scratches. I'm fine."

"And your Wilson is satisfied?"

Black Jack smiled, wondering if Wilson was ever really satisfied. "As much as he ever is."

"Then perhaps it is time you did something for yourself."

The comment surprised Hogan. "That's why I'm here."

"No. You are here because you think there is no other place you can go."

"Not another place that is as peaceful as this," Hogan agreed.

"I am not talking about peaceful. How about happy?"

Happy? The American didn't know what the Buddhist abbot was trying to tell him. "This is as happy as I get."

Mok Seng shook his head. "I looked in on you last night while you were sleeping. You were smiling happily then."

Hogan remembered he had been dreaming of Brom...and being together with Astrah in the tent, on the soft pillows.

"I had a nice dream for a change."

"Good. Then it is time that you left here for a while."

It seemed to Hogan that the monk was talking in riddles again. "And go where?"

Mok Seng reached under his robe and handed Hogan the krall. With a smile he answered, "You know where."

Hogan's face lit up as he stroked the weapon with his hand. "Yes. I know where."